MAJESTIC APARTMENT
MYSTERY

MAJESTIC APARTMENT
MYSTERY

Veda Taylor Strong

iUniverse, Inc.
Bloomington

MAJESTIC APARTMENT MYSTERY

iUniverse books may be ordered through booksellers or by contacting:

iUniverse
1663 Liberty Drive
Bloomington, IN 47403
www.iuniverse.com
1-800-Authors (1-800-288-4677)

ISBN: 978-1-4697-4510-7 (sc)
ISBN: 978-1-4697-4511-4 (ebk)

Printed in the United States of America

iUniverse rev. date: 01/25/2012

CONTENTS

CHAPTER 1

I was dreaming that the telephone was ringing. Why does it keep ringing? It should quit soon. I grabbed a pillow and put it over my head to block out the noise. That didn't help. Suddenly I sat straight up in bed, shaking my head as I realized that I was awake and the telephone was ringing nonstop. Apparently it had been ringing for a long time. Rolling over on my side, I grabbed for the house phone, knocking it from the nightstand onto the floor. Jumping out of bed I picked it up, hit the talk button, and unwittingly yelled, "hello!" There was not an immediate answer so I yelled hello again. This time I was sure the irritation could be heard in my voice. I looked at my digital alarm clock. It was only 2:47. Who could be calling so early in the morning? It had to be a wrong number. Why do wrong numbers always happen during the night? I was thinking of disconnecting and going back to bed, when the voice on the other end of the phone very softly asked for the apartment manager. It was so soft I had to listen carefully. I answered loudly that I was the manager and I asked the voice to talk louder. It seemed like forever before the voice started talking again, telling me about coming down the stairs and seeing a lady's arm sticking out between the railings under the stairs leading to the utility room.

I heard a click on the other end of the telephone as my caller hung up. I checked the phone to get a caller ID number but after checking the number I discovered the voice had called from a pay phone.

While I hurriedly threw on clothes and shoes I tried to figure out what was happening. This must be a hoax. Nothing ever happens around here. We are a very quiet respectable apartment building. I thought that I would check it out and then come back to bed. I grabbed my cell phone and put it in my pocket as I opened the door. Hurrying to the stairs and taking them two at a time I came to the landing that led to the utility room. There she was, just as the voice had described her to me. I immediately knelt down and picked up her wrist, and took her pulse. Her body was still warm leading me to believe that she had not been dead very long. In fact it must have just happened. Did the voice do this?

The lady was stretched full length on her back with one leg thrown over the other leg at the knee, and her long red hair fanned out over her head, where she had been carefully positioned. She was dressed as though she was going out to a fancy restaurant or maybe the opera. One delicate black spiked-heel shoe lay not far from her right foot but her left shoe was still on. As I looked, I noticed that she was not wearing jewelry. This seemed odd to me. Could this have been a robbery gone bad? I was very careful not to touch or walk through any thing. As I looked closer I could see blood coming from her hairline just above her left ear. The blood had run down and across the shoulder of a very expensive blue gown onto the floor. We had a murder on our hands. It was not as though I did not know my way around a crime scene. I had been police detective, Thomas Donavan for thirty years before retiring and becoming manager and part owner of this apartment complex.

I took pictures at different angles. No one needed to know about the pictures unless I was asked. I called 911. While I waited I looked for a gun or something out of the ordinary that could have caused the hole by her ear. It could not have been very big. I was still looking when I faintly heard the sirens, getting louder as they got closer. Soon the peacefulness was gone as the police took over.

As I stood there two detectives came forward and introduced themselves as Detectives Bill Hanley and Amy Taylor. They immediately started asking questions. After explaining what I knew, they wanted to know who had called me. I told them about the mystery voice. They looked as perplexed as me; surely this is what the caller meant to have happen. It certainly had me puzzled.

The victim was a very pretty red haired lady probably in her late twenties or early thirties. I recognized her as Cynthia Marquet from Baltimore, Maryland. She had moved into apartment 310 a few weeks ago, after moving to the Seattle area. She was employed by a large insurance firm in one of the tall high-rise buildings in down-town Seattle and her plans were to commute back and forth each day on the ferry.

My thoughts were soon interrupted by the noise being made by the police. People were looking out their apartment doors and a few came close enough to see what was happening. I had to ask them all to go back into their units, which they reluctantly did. Some of the doors never quite closed. Detective Taylor asked me several questions about Cynthia. I told her all I knew. A few minutes later she asked again just in case I remembered something. She took a card out of her pocket and handed it to me and let me know that I was to call her if I remembered anything at all. She wanted my cell phone number in case they needed to call with more questions. The whole area was being dusted for fingerprints. There was a lot of white powder on the telephone and around the landing. The police had been brushing and checking for fingerprints for quite some time. So many people used the landing, I thought it was useless to do this. Soon the coroner came with a crew and took over. He could not come up with a cause of death right away. Sure looked to me like she was shot and killed but I am sure they have to check out all possibilities. He started asking questions of the detectives and myself. I answered several questions over and over and I gave them my cell phone number. The body was gently put on a gurney and covered with a large white sheet, then carried down the stairs and out to a waiting coroner's vehicle and driven away. I was left with the impression that they would be coming back often to check the crime scene. The detectives and the police wanted to check out her apartment. Finding the door locked I stepped forward, unlocked it and threw the door open. Looking inside the apartment I found everything all very tidy and not a thing was out of place. The furniture was very nice but not real expensive. I really didn't know what they hoped to find. I was very interested and I wanted to be in on what ever was found. Following the detectives inside, Taylor stopped me and requested in a tone that would stop a wind storm, that I wait outside and advised me not to allow anyone to disturb the crime scene or the apartment. I was disappointed but I did as I was asked. Soon the detectives were back on the landing with folders of papers in their hands. One contained Cynthia's resume. Hanley explained to Taylor that he was not able to find a laptop or a purse. Taylor stated that she had not seen either of them. They decided that she must have had both and the items had gone with the murderer. He asked me if I knew any family members or close friends. I thought for a minute and explained that I had not seen anyone with her

Where was the gun or whatever was used to make the hole in her hairline? This was baffling. The weapon would have been close by if she had committed suicide. I was real sure that was not the case. When I had registered Cynthia into the apartment, she was very happy about being transferred to Seattle by her firm to take over an insurance department.

She had confided to me that she did not like living in the fast pace of Seattle's city life. Someone had told her about Bremington, so she had rented a car and spent the day looking over the town before deciding to stay. She had driven past the Majestic Apartments with its balconies and flowers and decided to check us out. We were not far from the ferries and she could walk to them for exercise.

I showed her a large two bedroom apartment with a water view. She loved everything about the apartment, immediately filling out the paper work, giving me the name of her employer and doing all the necessary things to rent this apartment. That was six weeks ago. After checking with her employer, I did not check her personal information further. I called her at her office and told her she could move in after she signed our contract.

Two days later, a large moving van loaded with furniture and her belongings arrived. The movers helped her set up the apartment. The next couple of days she spent getting settled in. She was happy and really looking forward to living in her apartment over looking the water.

She was a friendly warm person and I thought she was very down to earth for a person of her importance. The fellow tenants liked her and loved to talk to her about Baltimore among other things. She just seemed to fit in. Why would someone do this to her?

The detectives seemed to be very alert. Finding who had done this was going to be their priority. If they wanted my help, I would certainly do all I could. I knew I would be doing my own investigating.

CHAPTER 2

I opened the door to my apartment and went into the kitchen. The wall clock read 7:56 A.M. I had been gone for over five hours. It didn't seem that long but a lot had happened. Taking the coffeepot out of the cabinet, I automatically filled it with water and put coffee in the little strainer and plugged it in. While I waited for it to perk, I dropped into my easy chair. With the comfort of the chair and aroma of the coffee, I suddenly felt tired and drifted off to sleep. I dreamed of the crime scene and in my sleep I hashed it over step by step. Someone was watching me. I could feel their presence around the room. Immediately I felt in a panic telling myself this was nonsense. I was only having a nightmare. Sitting straight up in the chair, wide awake and alert, I found myself in a cold sweat. Pouring myself a mug of coffee, I stood looking out the window into the flower garden, trying hard to forget the morning by thinking of the flowers and the work that needed to be done. The garden entry was a beautiful rose arch. Going down a short path there were benches among the flowers. People spent hours sitting here reading or just relaxing, watching the different kinds of colorful fish in the large fish pond. Suddenly remembering the information I had promised the police and coroners' offices, I poured myself another mug of coffee. Carrying it into my office, I pulled Cynthia's folder from the filing cabinet. Sitting down at my desk and looking through the folder, I noticed there was not much more I could tell about her except that her emergency contact was Peggy Martin of Honolulu, Hawaii along with a telephone number she had given me. I looked for the name of her last employer but she had written "I will get the information for you." I replaced the panic and dreaded feelings with a feeling to do something. I would go question each of the tenants. Maybe they had remembered something different. First, I sat down and using the house phone, made calls to Detective Taylor and the coroners office, giving them Cynthia's friends name and phone number. I also explained what I knew about her employer. Basically they each thanked me and asked me to call back if I remembered anything else. They were both very closed mouthed and I could not get either of them to reveal a thing.

Deciding that now would be a good time to talk to the tenants, I left my apartment and went upstairs, I started with Apartment Number One across from Number Ten, Cynthia's apartment. I knocked on the door and the tenant, an elderly man named

Harry Kingsley opened it immediately. He asked me inside, and pointed for me to sit down on the big overstuffed sofa in his living room. After I had refused his offer of coffee, I asked him if he had seen or heard anything across the hall. Maybe a door closing, someone talking, or maybe someone using the stairs. He had not heard or seen a thing.

I continued from unit to unit until I came to Unit Nine next door to Cynthia. A lady in her sixties by the name of Martha Mailer lived here. I knocked on the door waited a few seconds and knocked again. I was about to leave when she barely opened the door enough for me to speak to her. We stood like this for a minute making small talk. I asked her if I could come in. She was hesitant but opened the door, standing back and letting me pass. She then shut the door and locked it behind me. I thought this was strange behavior. She asked me into her very neat kitchen where she sat me down at her table with a red-checkered table cloth. Her apartment looked out over the driveway and water the same as Cynthia's. I walked to the window, and looked outside all around as far as I could see. Maybe somebody could have climbed up the balconies but it would have been dangerous. I asked her the same questions I had asked the others. She was very nervous, shaken up, as though she knew something. I told her that the only people I would tell would be the police. She had a panic attack and begged me not to say anything. She was very upset and definitely worried. She blurted out that Cynthia uncle, Jack Roma. It needed an immediate signature and she was to hurry back with it.

Her Uncle Jack was different and she was always afraid of him but this was part of her job. After parking in front of her uncles' store she went inside. Looking around she did not see him so she went on into the back room thinking he was there. The back door was open so she went closer and from that time on she wished she had not. Jack was standing with a gun pointed at a man known as Mister Garcia. He pulled the trigger, blood began flowing from his face and Mister Garcia fell dead on the ground. Jack yelled and two large muscular men came and grabbed the dead man as Jack looked up and saw her at the door. She was not very quiet as she rushed back through the store to her car. Opening the door, she jumped in and drove off as fast as she could. Looking in the rearview mirror she saw her uncle hurrying back into the store.

Against her fathers advice, she went to the police and told them what she had seen. Jack was arrested and the outcome of the trial depended on her. She took the stand and told the truth about what she had seen. This along with other crimes, put her uncle in jail for many years. Some how he was out after only one year. Some say he bribed a judge and others say that he owned the judicial system. Jack had called her father and told him that he was going to kill her if he could find her. Her dad immediately gave her a lot of money, several new identities and sent her to Florida where he thought she would be safe.

There she took an apartment close to Disney World thinking she could get lost in the crowds. One day while there and deciding it was safe, she put in her application at the Disney office using one of her new identities, Rose Rosellini. They liked her resume' and she was hired two weeks later. The work was not easy but she worked hard and after four years was rising to the top. She was next in line for a promotion. One day she received a call from her father. He was in the lobby of her building and wanted her to come down and meet him. It was very important. Getting permission from her supervisor she took the afternoon off and met with her father. Finding a little cafe close by, they ordered lunch. While they waited, she asked him what was so important. He told her that Jack had come to his house and questioned her mother about Cynthia. When he could not get answers, he left in a bad mood threatening everyone. Three days later her mother was crossing a street that she had crossed all of her life and was run over and killed by an unknown driver. He felt it was Jack's revenge. Of course the police called it an accidental death caused by person or persons unknown. Being afraid for his daughter and only child, he suggested that she leave Florida right away. He handed her another envelope with more money and a plane ticket to Alaska. She felt horrified and grief stricken about her mother and did not want to leave her dad. She did not want to go, but knew that her father was right. She said goodbye and hugged him not knowing if she would ever see him again. This was the hardest thing she ever had to do.

She went to her supervisor and told him that she had to leave her job because of an emergency. He offered her time off but she declined. She knew she would not be coming back. She then went to the cashier and drew her pay. At her apartment, she took only a change of clothes in a purse-like bag with her money and her new IDs. Two men approached her as she was leaving. She was ready to run but they blocked her way. One told her that they were FBI agents and were asked to keep track of her. She thought it was something that her father had done. Jack was wanted for a lot of crimes and hoped they could arrest him. She was given a business card with two names each having a phone number and was told to always keep this card no matter what happened. If she was in trouble call one or the other and they would be there.

Just outside her building, she caught a taxi to the airport. While riding, she kept watching out the windows for anyone acting out of character. Before long, she was aboard a flight on her way out of Florida and hopefully into a good life like the one she had just left.

Arriving in Anchorage in the late afternoon, not knowing the city, she decided to get a room close to the airport. She spent the next day resting and looking in the phone book for possible work places. She began calling the different fish companies along the wharf. She thought that nobody would think to look for her there. She had called several places to no avail. She was beginning to think that she had not chosen a good plan when one of her calls found an owner wanting a person to take care of an office and keep books. She met Midge, a co-worker at her office. They became very good friends. Midge was a very petite person and it was easy to guess her nick name. She had a house and asked Cynthia to share it. Agreeing to pay the utilities she moved in. They often went to a tavern called 'The Whaler'. They would only stay a couple hours. The tavern became wild and unruly after nine at night and it was no place for them. They also spent time outside Anchorage in snow country working with the trained racing dogs destined to go with their masters on the Iditarod. They got to be well known and the animals loved them.

Life was interesting and fun. She was hidden in plain sight and hopefully her worries were over. After being there for three years and coming home from work one evening, she found the back door standing wide open. She was afraid to go in. Her neighbor came to her and told her that a man fitting Jack's description had been there and Midge had invited him in. Cynthia knew that he had convinced Midge that he was in town just to see his niece that he adored and missed. Otherwise he would not have gotten in. Going into the living room she found her only friend lying in a pool of blood. While she held her head, Midge told Cynthia that her uncle Jack had beaten her because she would not tell him where she worked. He probably would have killed her but someone had knocked on the door and scared him away. Jumping up she called for an ambulance. Kneeling down again she grabbed a pillow from the sofa behind her, and laid Midge's head on it. While they waited Cynthia told her that she was leaving and would not be back. She also told her a little bit about uncle Jack so she would be aware. She wished she had told her before. The ambulance arrived putting her only friend on a gurney and took her to the hospital. Again she packed a change of clothing, her new IDs and money into a big bag. Just as she was leaving, a car came to a stop in front of the house. She cautiously looked out the window for fear that Jack had come back. To her surprise, one of the men getting out of the car was one of the FBI agents that she had seen in Florida. They always seemed to show up when there was a tragedy or something had happened. They sat down while Cynthia told them what had just gone on. She was very reluctant to stay and talk. They told her that her father was found drowned in his bathtub. The coroner declared it was a homicide. At that time the FBI starting watching her again, but were too late to save her friend from the terrible beating. They took her to the airport and watched while she bought a ticket to Honolulu, Hawaii. Soon the people were called to board the plane. The last she saw of Alaska was the FBI agents watching her back as she boarded.

She rented a room in downtown Honolulu away from the beaches. She knew she had to find a job. She still had most of her father's money and had saved a large amount from her wages but knew she had to be kept busy and find employment. She asked the cashiers at her hotel if there was any work and where she would go to find it. Nothing was accomplished by this. She thought of the big pineapple fields. She rented a car and drove around asking about work. She left her new name and a new cell phone number so she could be called. It was not long before a call came from an office manager at an insurance firm in downtown Honolulu. This was great. She was real excited about it and it was her kind of work. She felt very confident and comfortable there for six years avoiding the public eye as much as she possibly could. Then a man came by her work and asked to see her. The receptionist did not like to bother her. Only by showing his FBI credentials, would the receptionist let Cynthia know. He was then escorted into her very large, fancy office. She sat behind her desk while he sat down in a chair facing her. He had come to tell her that Jack and his henchmen, had been seen on Waikiki beach and around Honolulu. They were showing an older photograph of her and asking if anyone knew her. It would not be long before she was found. Jack was not going to give up. She and the FBI decided that in some way he was demented. She just could not believe it. The tears came and she wept. She was a good person. Why was he still on the loose. She dried her eyes knowing the answers as well as anyone. The FBI men were able to find her easy enough. This time they took her to the airport and watched while she bought a ticket for Seattle. Arriving there, she rented a hotel room for two weeks in the newly formed town of Sea-Tac, across from the airport. She immediately bought a Seattle Times newspaper. When she had arrived in the hotel lobby, she noticed a computer and printer for the use of the guests. The first day she wrote out a resume' using another alias and ID. Using the hotel printer she made several copies. Looking through the phone book, she copied the names of insurance and legal firms and their e-mails. She sent resumes by e-mail and regular mail to companies needing office workers. She went through the want ads in the paper and on the computer. She found a mail slot next to the counter and bought stamped envelopes from the hotel clerk. She felt that she had a good chance of finding work.

The next day, the phone started ringing and she had several offers of jobs. She spent another several days going from one interview another. Finally she was offered a department of her own at an insurance company in a high rise building in Seattle. She never gave me her real name or where she was from. She did say that she had never been in Baltimore. She had heard so much about it that she thought it would be a good cover story. She was afraid to get close to anyone for fear they would be hurt or killed. She advised me to speak to her only in passing. She convinced me that she really did have to live like this.

A few days later Cynthia mentioned that she had met a nice man through her work. Jason worked for another firm but they had gotten acquainted. She *was getting up the courage to go out with him some evening. They seemed to have a lot in common.*

"Did Cynthia give a description of Jason? Did she mention the name of his firm?"

Martha shook her head no. "Cynthia just said he was a nice person and worked for G.A.G. H. Life Insurance."

I held Martha for a while longer and I assured her that she was safe here. I was in awe of her story and I understood her fear when I knocked at the door.

Advising her not to answer the door or telephone, I also told her to pack a good sized suitcase. She had a look of bewilderment on her face. I told her the police may put her under-cover somewhere. I stood up and headed for the door. I could hear the dead bolt hit home as she locked the door behind me.

CHAPTER 3

Immediately I called the station and asked for Hanley or Taylor. It seemed a long time before Hanley came on the line. I told him who I was and that it would be worth his time to come to my apartment right away letting him know that I had discovered some important information on the Cynthia Marquet case and I could only give it to him if he came to me. He was not happy, made loud noises and grunted but said that he would be over.

In the meantime, I went back to the murder scene. I ducked under the crime tape still surrounding it. Looking to where Cynthia was found dead my imagination and instincts took over. I pictured someone or maybe two people placing her there and making sure she was laid out properly. I tried to picture from which way the murderer had come with her but the scene was very clean leaving no clues. Was she killed in her unit, or up the stairs or maybe in the elevator.

By the time I got back to my place, Hanley and Taylor were both there. I asked them in and they sat in my kitchen and I relayed the story as close as I could to what Martha had told me. They sat in amazement and waited until I had finished, and then they erupted with questions. They would have to wait for answers from Martha.

I told them that Martha was very scared and was afraid to stay here as long as the killer was on the loose. I made them promise me that they would do all they could to move her somewhere else for safety until the case was solved. I called to let Martha know that we were on the way to see her.

When I got to her door I rang the bell and also knocked. I could hear the key in the lock and the dead bolt spring back. She opened the door and grabbed me by the sleeve pulling me into her apartment and the detectives followed. She stood by the door and locked it again with the dead bolt and key.

She invited us to sit around on chairs in the living room while she disappeared into the kitchen and brought us glasses of lemonade. She had hardly sat down before Hanley introduced himself and Taylor, then he asked her to repeat to them what she had told me.

She looked at me hesitantly. I nodded then went and sat beside her on the couch. She repeated almost word for word what she had told me. She had not left anything out. She also told them that she was very afraid and wanted to go some place until the person responsible for this was caught and put in jail.

The detectives told us that they had wired Honolulu and the reply came back that the friends name and phone number were bogus.

Martha got up and went into her bedroom bringing her large beige leather purse back with her. She sat back down with the purse on her lap and unzipped it. She gave me the card that Cynthia had given her. The one with the FBI agents names and the two phone numbers. Taylor was already reaching for it.

I pulled it back out of her reach and asked her what their plan was for Martha's safety. It was not safe for her to stay at her apartment. Taylor walked away and made a phone call. She came back and told us she had gotten permission from their captain to put Martha in the Holiday Hotel until this mess was all over.

I spoke up and offered to take Martha in my car. It would not be good to drop her off in a police car. They had a discussion and decided I was right. Taylor had to go to the station house for some things and would meet us there. Martha was registered under the name of Barbara Anderson.

I handed Taylor the card with the agents names and phone numbers which I had managed to memorize until I could write them down. After reading it, she turned it over and over in her hand. This is a different kind of paper she remarked. She showed me a very fine almost unnoticeable wire through the lettering. This is how the FBI kept track of her. She carried it in her wallet. Cynthia never knew it was there. The detectives were discussing the card as they left the apartment building.

Turning to Martha, I asked her if she had packed. She took me into her bedroom where two large suitcases sat full, and ready to go. I grabbed the suitcases by the handles, one in each hand, as Martha grabbed her coat, purse and a large bag, I followed her dragging the suitcases on the wheels. After we were outside, she locked her apartment door and the dead bolt with her key. She told me that nobody would get in.

I loaded the suitcases in my car and we took off. While we drove we watched the traffic around us for anything suspicious. When we reached the hotel, I drove around to see if everything was in place. I went with her, to the registration desk and while she checked in, I checked out the lobby. An elderly couple sat reading but nothing seemed out of the ordinary.

Martha registered under Barbara Anderson and had her keycard in her hand. I went to the room with her and scanned it very carefully. Leaving her to lock the door behind me, I went to the car and brought up her luggage. While I was waiting for her to unlock the door, I looked around. All seemed to be quiet in the hallway.

She seemed nervous as I entered her room. Apparently the phone had been ringing but she did not answer it. She had been cautioned not to.

I decided to wait around and see if it rang again, which it did. I answered and the receptionist told me that a detective was on her way up. Looking out the little round peep-hole in the door, I saw Taylor. I opened the door and when she came in, she handed a large envelope to Martha with everything she needed, including Taylor's business card. There was also a cell phone she could use to contact her family and friends. She absolutely was not to tell anyone her new name, phone number or where she was. This would be a dangerous thing for her to do.

Taylor told her that from now on she was to answer only to Barbara. We would all be calling her Barbara. A policeman in plain clothes would be close by at all times. There would be no need for him to contact her unless it was important. There would be three of them, each taking eight hour shifts. The day guy would only be known by code A, the afternoon guy would be code B and the night time guy would be code C. She would never know their true names.

After we had her settled, we both left together. I explained that I had looked everything over and all looked good. We talked about what a shame it was to have to move her. We knew Jack Roma would have people all around if he had a hint that Martha knew these things and maybe more. He would certainly be after her. We do not know what, if anything that Cynthia had told anyone.

It did not make any difference how careful plans were made, Jack always seemed to know or was able to find out anything he wanted to know. It was almost as though he had unworldly talents. Knowing that this was not true, we decided that he was a very clever man. The police had been alerted all around the globe. He seemed to evade traps set for him. It was as though he wore a disguise. I have been told that the best place to hide is in plain sight. If this is true, Jack could be any where. He would not go back to New York with all the federal warrants. We were fairly sure of that.

Taylor stopped for a minute and turned to face me. She told me that although she was not suppose to say anything, she felt that I was part of this mystery.

Her and Hanley had been combing the different pawn shops looking for the laptop and jewelry. They got a lead from a lady that works at a place called Ron's on Sixth and Marian. They learned from her that a laptop computer and a diamond set, consisting of earrings, pendant and ring, had just been pawned. They could not do a thing about it until Ron, the owner came in.

As I drove home, I could not believe the events of the past two days. I had not expected to do detective work again, but I had not lost my touch. I just hoped we could catch this person, or persons, very soon before someone else got hurt.

Since Taylor had mentioned that they had a lead on the laptop and jewelry, maybe I would go snooping around. Getting into my car, I drove to Ron's Pawn Shop. I arrived at the same time as Taylor did. She wanted to know why I was there. I jokingly told her that two heads were better than one. She laughed and motioned for me to follow her.

The guy behind the counter was a big man with a beard. He had a very gravely voice and a very bad disposition. He asked if he could help us. Taylor stepped forward and showed her badge and his attitude changed. She asked about a laptop and a set of jewelry consisting of a very expensive diamond necklace and earring set. She had reason to believe that he had recently bought the items. She explained to him that it was part of a murder scene. He stuttered for a minute and then went to his back room and brought forward a blue velvet case containing a beautiful teardrop diamond pendant with matching earrings. He walked into a small room on the other side and brought back a laptop that he placed beside the jewelry. Taylor told him that they were believed to be stolen property. She asked him to tell us all about the items and not to leave anything out.

He said that a young man about eighteen or nineteen years of age had come into the store with only the laptop. He told him that it was his but he needed some money so decided to pawn it. Ron did not think a thing about it. A lot of people were doing the same thing. He gave him a hundred dollars for it.

The jewelry was a different story. The same person came back and he waited awhile and looked around. He then came up to the Ron and showed him the diamonds. He wanted to know what they were worth. Ron checked them out and saw they were perfect blue tinged diamonds worth several thousand dollars. The guy did not seem to know what he had so he only give him three hundred dollars for the set. He took the money leaving his name and phone number as he had before. Taylor asked for a copy. The name was Tad Warren and his address was not far away. Taylor gave Ron her card and told him to call her if the guy came back. She went back to her car and got a standard police receipt. She wrote down the items, dated and signed it. While handing Ron the receipt, she informed him that she would be taking the items to the police station as evidence.

Ron was glad to hear that he was not in trouble and told Taylor that he would help in anyway that he could. He should have known the pieces were stolen but he just ignored the thought.

CHAPTER 4

I went back to the crime scene. No one had been there. I gave thoughts to what might have happened. I tried to picture a person carrying Cynthia's body. She was not a big person. Possibly 120 pounds but I know that dead weight is heavy. How far had he carried her?

I went outside and attempted to climb the terraces to her second floor apartment. I am over six feet tall and I reached as far as I could but I was several inches away from touching Cynthia's landing. This could not be accomplished even with a ladder. With some one carrying someone and the amount of noise it would make caused me to rule out transporting the body in this manner.

I grabbed a big carved piece of wood from the garden. It was unwieldy and heavy. This is what I needed to experiment. I stooped down and picked it up carrying it to where I put it down to open the door. I picked it back up and carried it inside again putting it down to close the door. I picked it back up and started to carry it up stairs but it was so heavy that I had to put it down to rest. Shortly, I had reached the landing and put it down where she had been laying. The experiment showed me that the noise of stopping, opening and closing the door, and generally being there would have been heard by someone. Either someone is keeping very quiet or she wasn't carried. I ruled this possibility out, too.

After returning the wood to the garden and putting it where I had gotten it from, I sat on a bench and just let my mind wander. Maybe I should check out the elevator. It was old and very noisy and just maybe someone would remember hearing it. After I got onto the elevator and went to the third floor, I looked across eighty feet to apartment number 310. This seemed almost as impossible.

The only thing I could think of was she was either killed in her apartment or she was enticed to climb over the railing where she was killed. There was no sign of a struggle. Nor was there any blood but where she laid. Maybe she had been drugged. The detectives had gone through the apartment thoroughly. Nothing seemed out of place and there was not a sign of blood.

My final assumption was that she had let somebody she knew into her apartment. Maybe they had drinks and hers was drugged. Someone could have walked her out of her apartment crossing the hall where she was talked into going over the railing. Maybe they took something of hers and put it there and she was retrieving it but was killed instead.

I looked in every little hole around the scene. I was beginning to think that the killer had taken the weapon and everything with it when I stepped on something. Using my handkerchief I reached down and picked it up. It was a piece of hard wood the size of a small pea covered with blood. I must have pushed it out of its hiding place. This had to be what killed her but how was it done? How was the wooden pea shot into her head? I put the pea in my handkerchief so it would not get lost. This was an enigma that had to be solved.

I was getting very excited. Standing for a couple minutes with my thoughts on what was I looking for that would shoot the pea, I started to turn around when everything went black. I woke up with tenants standing close by. An ambulance had been sent for and an EMT was standing over me. He kept talking to me when all I wanted was for him to do was just be quiet. Why was he so loud? I had a bad headache. I finally came around and attempted to sit up. My head was throbbing like a jack hammer. When I asked what happened I was told that somebody had hit me in the head with a hard object and that I had been out for awhile. A report had been made and the police were sent for.

Taylor and Hanley showed up and asked me all kinds of questions. I told them that I could not tell anything with everybody standing around. The landing was cleared of the people. The EMT thought

I should go to the hospital and have myself checked out for a concussion. I refused to go and suddenly he was gone too.

Getting Taylor by herself, so I could explain about the experiments I had completed, was a feat in its own. She was very busy, and professional about her work. Finally she stopped and asked me how I felt as she smiled and touched my forehead.

I told her everything up until I went back to the murder scene. Then I told her that I might have found out how she was killed and part of the murder weapon. The person who attacked me was after this. I reached for my pocket and handkerchief. Where is my handkerchief I asked as I was getting a panicky feeling. Someone had turned my pockets inside out looking for something and my bunched handkerchief lay off to the side with my wallet, keys and some change. I picked it up and spread it open and there was the bloody pea. It had been over looked by who ever had hit me. I'm sure this was what they wanted. Handing it to Taylor I let her know that she was in charge of it now. She had to be careful.

While I was there looking, I did not see nor did I hear anyone else there. They could not have been there long or they would have seen me put something into my handkerchief. Now someone would be after me for sure. I will not be scared away from here but I will be very vigilant. No one will sneak up on me again.

I got to my feet and the room seemed to be turning around. Hanley grabbed me and sat me down again until I could get over my weak knees. I was hit hard enough to knock me out. I am glad he or she did not stay around to finish the job.

In the mean time, Ron from the pawn shop had called Taylor and told her that the guy we wanted had come back to pawn a beautiful diamond ring and was still there. He would try to hold him there if she could come right away.

They both took off in a hurry. I got to my feet holding my head with one hand and the banister with the other. I was going to my apartment to rest. I was sure that Taylor would fill me in on what they found at the pawn shop.

I took some aspirin and laid down on the bed and stretched out. It felt so good. I thought I would stay right here for ever or at least until the pounding quit in my head. I wonder what I was hit with. I should have looked for something but my head hurt to bad.

Taylor called to tell me that they picked up the guy at the pawn shop along with the diamond ring. They were holding him at the station. They were about to start questioning him but she decided to call me first. She was keeping me in the loop.

She wanted to know how I was feeling? Would I check on Martha tonight if I felt up to it? I looked at the clock and it was 7:30. I did not realize that it was that late. I must have been out longer than I thought.

The pain in my head had eased up a lot. It would not take long to see Martha and then I could come back to bed. I was exhausted. Fixing myself a sandwich from a ham I had cooked yesterday I sat down at the table and ate it with a glass of cold milk. It tasted like a gourmet meal. This would hold me until I got back home.

Taking my jacket from the hook, and putting on my Mariners hat, I went out the door locking it firmly behind me. All the while I kept watching for something out of place or different. I wish I knew what it was. I was sure of one thing. I was being watched and I did not like the feeling.

Driving the opposite direction from the Holiday Hotel I pulled into a grocery store parking lot. Going inside, I walked around, stopping and taking a bottle of coke out of the cooler. I paid for the coke, drinking it as I watched out the window and chatted with the clerk. Nothing changed and no one seemed to be following me so I got into my car and headed toward the hotel and Martha.

I kept a look out and studied each car around me. Just a block from the hotel I spied a little dress shop. Pulling into one of the three parking spaces, I parked, got out and locked up. I decided to walk around the shop into the alley and watch for a while to see if I was alone. Nothing was happening so I walked on down the alley and into the hotels back door. Again I stood watching but nothing happened. Then I got on the elevator and went up to Martha's room.

I knocked on her door listening for movement inside. I was starting to worry when I heard her opening the door, letting the automatic lock click behind us. Nothing had happened. She had called room service and they had brought her a very nice dinner. Other than watching television and crocheting, she had not heard nor seen anything. She was going to call it a night and go to bed. It had been a very exhausting day for everyone. I gave her my cell phone number in case she needed something.

I decided not to tell her about my experience at the crime scene. Maybe some day when this is all over we could talk about it. After telling her good night I left, watching her door for a while but all seemed quiet so I got into the elevator and went down stairs and retraced my steps to the back door.

Hearing glass breaking near the dress shop, I started to run toward my car and there stood a guy about my size with a crowbar in his hand breaking the drivers side window of my new car. I grabbed the crowbar meaning to hit him with it. Surprisingly, he let go of it. Thinking better of this, I threw the crowbar away from us and threw a punch at his nose instead. I connected and he fell backwards with blood dripping down his chin. I was fairly sure that I broke it. Getting his posture back he came for me with fear in his eyes. I side-stepped him and he turned and swung, hitting my head and I felt the jack hammers going off again in my head. I waited for him to come at me again and I swung with everything I had, straight at his jaw. He was out for the count. Feeling good about myself I thought, not bad for an old guy. I still had what it took.

I called Taylor at home. I told her the whole story. While I waited for her to join me I looked him over. I had never seen him before. He was Latino, my size but several years younger. He started to move and get up. I told him to stay where he was. I had picked up the crowbar and held it so he knew I meant business. I wanted to interrogate him but I knew if he was arrested he would holler and probably be released on a technicality. I left it up to Taylor.

At this time of the night, people are not around and it is good not to draw a crowd. While keeping an eye on the prisoner, I was watching around me in case someone unknown was there.

Taylor and Hanley showed up together in a unmarked car along with two police officers in a patrol car. They, tried to question the guy but he could not speak English. He only repeated the name Pedro Gomez. He was not carrying identification. Hanley put him into the patrol car and the detectives took him away. They would find out who he was and why he was damaging my car when they got him to the station.

Reaching through the broken window, I unlocked the door, brushing as much glass off the seat as I could into a plastic bag that the wind had blown up against the curb. Nothing I could do about the broken glass on the ground except pick up the big pieces. I threw the bag into the large green dumpster in the alley, got into my car and headed for home. Anything else would have to wait until morning. Right now the jack hammers were back at work in my head and I needed more aspirin and my bed. I knew by morning I would definitely be hurting.

I was still watching my back as I opened my apartment door. Nobody seemed to be around. So I quickly closed it. I looked around the unit to be sure all was well there. Then I headed for the bathroom cabinet and the aspirin. I took three and then got into my pajamas and into bed. While thinking of a good nights sleep the house phone rang. I had thoughts of clicking the off button and laying it down but curiosity would not let me. I answered with a 'hello' and waited for a reply. The same soft voice had returned. It told me that I was doing a great job as detective. Again the phone went dead.

CHAPTER 5

I was just finishing breakfast when Taylor called. I told her about my strange phone call. Although I was listening closely, I was not able to figure who it was or really why I was called. It still remains a mystery.

The guy breaking into my car could not speak English, Taylor told me. They had called in a police interpreter and were told that Gomez was going to steal the car and find work around Omak or Wenatchee in the fruit orchards. Hanley was finishing up the paper work to send him to Seattle.

Guess I will have to call my insurance agent to turn in a claim. Taylor told me that she would see to it that I got a copy of the police report.

Before grilling Todd Warren for the theft of the laptop and jewelry, Taylor read him his rights asking him if he wanted an attorney. He said he was not guilty of anything. No, he did not want an attorney. He was not being cooperative in any way so Hanley decided to give another technique a try. They left him alone in the interrogation room for two hours, checking on him once in a while. He was getting more and more nervous. This is what Hanley wanted. Finally he opened the door and went into the room. A guard was called to escort Todd into the restroom. It was not long before he was setting back down across the table. The detective sat there quietly for several minutes looking through papers in a folder giving Todd more time to squirm and wonder what the folders were about.

He began by telling Todd that the theft of the laptop and jewelry made him the prime suspect for the murder of Cynthia Marquet, the owner of the items. He would be held and charged for murder as well as theft. He would be in prison for life or until he was a very old man. Hanley gave him another chance to speak up but received only silence. A guard was called to take him to jail where he would be booked on one count of murder and two counts of theft. Hanley stood up and headed for the door.

Todd yelled for him to wait. He wanted to talk. Sitting back down across the table from him Hanley asked him if he was thirsty then told the guard to bring them each a coke. Denying he had anything to do with either crime Todd began by telling how he got involved. He was walking close to the apartments one night about eleven o'clock heading for the Seattle ferry. He had just gotten off work and having the next two days off he decided to visit a friend in Seattle. He heard the lid of a dumpster hit a wall. Out of curiosity he looked into the alley, toward the noise and noticed a tall well dressed man standing there. He watched for a while and saw him throw away a laptop, a bag, a small box that could have been jewelry and objects from his pockets and a purse. Taking off plastic gloves, he threw them in too.

Todd waited for the man to leave. He hoped he had not been seen when the man turned and faced him. Nothing happened and the man went around the end of the building and vanished down the street. He then climbed into the dumpster and retrieved the items looking them over real good thinking he had hit a jackpot. He kept the jewelry and lap top throwing everything else back into the dumpster. He decided to pawn them and get some money. He had not given a thought to where they had come from.

Hanley asked why he had not come clean before now and saving every one a lot of time and effort. His explanation was that he did not want the guy to come back and possibly recognize him. He kept denying over and over again that he had anything to do with any murder or theft. The items had been thrown away. This should mean something.

Taylor asked if he thought he could work with a sketch artist. It was getting dark but Todd thought he had gotten a good look at him. After Hanley had called in a sketch artist, he got up and walked to the water cooler where a few policemen were standing. He told one of them to bring Todd to his desk. He sent two of the cops to go through the dumpster where the diamonds were found, explaining that they were looking for a woman's purse, and a pair of plastic gloves. It was a long shot but maybe they would find something.

He saw Taylor and asked her what had been found on the laptop that could help. Taylor replied that the hard drive was completely erased but the lab people were trying to find some way to bring some of it back. It was just a maybe. No promises.

Todd was brought in and sat down at Hanley's desk. The artist came and sat with him and they kept busy for a long time. Finally Todd told them that the sketch was absolutely the man he saw at the dumpster. The sketch artist left and Hanley had come back. He questioned Todd further since seeing the sketch of the man. It might bring back something else that he had maybe forgotten.

The policemen returned from the dumpster with a soiled purse and a pair of plastic gloves. They were not very happy and they smelled from going through the dumpster. Their long shot had come through. The purse held Cynthia's wallet with folding money and her identification. Hanley took the evidence and turned it over to the lab. She believed Todd's story all along but now she was sure. If he had stolen the items he surely would have taken the large amount of folding money from the wallet.

Todd had to go before the judge the next morning. The detectives had a talk between themselves and decided that Todd was telling the truth. He really was a nice kid and was just in the right place at the wrong time.

The next morning both detectives were in court to put in a good word for him. Several people had been called before the judge and now Todd Warren was being called. He arose walking to the bench, standing before the judge he was asked to tell his story. After he was finished Taylor and Hanley were called to come forward and they each told what they had concluded. The judge looked through the folder in front of him and looking up at Todd he told him that he felt as the detectives did. He did not believe that he was a criminal. It was a weird event and Todd had responded to it. The judge asked Todd if he could stay out of trouble if he was released. Todd was very nervous as he immediately answered, "Yes sir."

The judge then told him that he had six months to repay Ron at the pawn shop. When this was done, he would bring a receipt back to the judge and would then be released of all liability. He was told to stop at the clerks desk and get an appointment for six months later then he was free to go. He shook hands with Taylor and Hanley telling them he would be available if needed. With a big smile on his face he about fell over his own feet trying to leave the court in a hurry.

(HAPTER 6

Taylor was on the phone asking questions from the different insurance companies. It seemed that the G.A.G.H. insurance that Martha had brought up was situated in downtown Seattle, also in a high rise building some where. For some reason an address or telephone number could not be found. They had no idea where to start looking for him. It might be with other insurance offices under the name of a corporation. Hanley and Taylor would take the next ferry to Seattle with a picture of Cynthia and a sketch of the alleged thief and see if they could connect him as Jason or connect him with Cynthia in any way. They had no idea where he had been working. The plan was to leave on the 11:30 ferry for Seattle and check out all the insurance companies in the downtown area. This could take most of the afternoon. Hopefully they would come back with a lot of information and answers.

I was entering the neighborhood supermarket when a man about my age followed me inside. While standing at the ice cream freeze trying to

43

decide on a flavor, the same man came towards me looking very intent and asked if I was Thomas Donavan? Always very hesitant to give my name I asked him who wanted to know. He showed me his FBI badge and credentials telling me his name was Robert Devon. He had seen the murder story and Cynthia's picture in a news paper. The place of the murder was mentioned. This is why he had been following me. He had stayed away until he was sure that he would not be interfering. The detectives and I were doing an excellent job. Indicating that he would not be there long he cautioned me not to reveal to anyone that we had met or had a conversation. He was working under cover and it would be just as well that no one knew. I told him all I knew except for the little wooden ball with blood on it. This was crucial information. Let Hanley or Taylor tell him if they wanted him to know.

He said he would contact the detectives and get copies of the pictures. Maybe put them in the New York Times. Might get some kind of lead from it. He knew that Cynthia's real name was Sandra Roma from the south side of New York City. He repeated what Martha had told him. The story she had told Martha was true. Her father, Michael Roma, had turned himself in to the FBI. For his freedom and watching out for his daughter he had agreed to tell all. There were several sessions with him before word was leaked out and Michael was found dead in his bathtub. Not much doubt that Jack was involved. The FBI had put Robert on the case from the very beginning. He asked if we had found a card with names and phone numbers on it? This was their way of keeping track of her. I suggested that he talk to Taylor. Walking away he let me know that he would be talking to me soon. I was shocked to think that I was being followed by the FBI. More than likely I would learn a lot more later.

I completed my shopping paid for my purchases and was heading for my car when my cell phone starting ringing. I let it ring while I unlocked and opened the car door. I put the groceries on the back seat and stepped back a few feet to answer the telephone when the earth seemed to come up and hit me. I was blown backward about fifty feet, hitting the ground with an enormous thud. People came running from every direction. Soon a large crowd had gathered around me. My car was a fireball sending large flames, smoke and the smell of gasoline into the sky. It was as though I was watching a movie from the balcony of a theater. I was in and out of reality not knowing for sure where I was. Hearing sirens coming towards me from the police cars, fire trucks and at least one ambulance, I felt like I was having another dream. I was lifted onto a gurney and was on my way to the hospital in a matter of minutes. I tried to ask questions but an oxygen mask was placed over my face.

Waking up and falling back to sleep until finally I became fully awake and discovered I was in a hospital room. Looking around I saw that I was alone. Someone had undressed me and put me into a night shirt. As I laid there I tried to remember what had happened. Then it all came back to me with a jolt. My car had been bombed and I was suppose to be dead. It came to me that my cell phone had been ringing.

A large no nonsense nurse came in and asked if I was comfortable. She put an IV in my arm and gave me some pills to make me feel better. She told me the doctor would be coming in and talking to me. No matter what I asked her, the answer was the same. The pills must have knocked me out. When I awoke, a different nurse was tending to me. She said she was glad to see me awake. I had been sleeping for nearly twenty-four hours. After asking if I was hungry, she left to get something for me to eat.

Taylor came through the door asking me if I could afford to take time off like this. She was grinning ear to ear. In her hand was a large milk shake which she handed to me while she told me that it was good for me. After we went through the niceties she told me that she was worried. I let her know that I was glad to see her, too. A familiar face in a sea of unknowns. She told me what I already knew. A bomb had been planted under the drivers seat and was set up so it would go off as soon as he turned the key in the ignition. If he had gotten right into the car and started the engine up, he would not be here to talk about it. Somehow the telephone had set it off saving his life.

She told me that a Robert Devon from the FBI had been to see her and Hanley at the precinct. I told her that I had told him everything except for the bloody wooden ball. She said that she had not told him either. We would keep that quiet for awhile.

I asked her about her trip to Seattle. After driving off the ferry and going to the addresses they had looked up the night before, they walked for an hour going to about every insurance company in down town Seattle. They showed the pictures to everyone that would look at them. They were about to quit when a lady told them where to find the G.A.G.H. Insurance company. The directions took them to the building next door. Going to the twelfth floor on the elevator, they walked to suite 23. There it was with the letters on the door. Why was it so hard to find?

They opened the door and walked up to the receptionists desk. Then asked if there was a Jason working there. Much to their surprise, the lady pushed a button on the telephone and was told to usher them into the office. They looked at each other and followed the receptionist. A tall slender man came from behind a large mahogany desk towards them. He shook their hands and asked them to be seated in two overstuffed chairs facing the desk. He wanted to know who they were and what they wanted him for. He was an executive and did not work as a salesman. He did not come into contact with many people. They told him their names while showing their badges.

Hanley asked if he knew Cynthia Marquet? He said he had met her at an insurance meeting. They seemed to hit it off and hoped to get together for dinner some time. Taylor stepped in and told Jason that Cynthia had been murdered and they were investigating the homicide. They showed him the police sketch but he did not know anything about the man in the sketch. There was no doubt that Jason was telling the truth. The detectives stood up and thanked him. They gave them their cards and asked him to call if he thought of anything more.

They then went to the Gemini Insurance Company. Showing a picture of Cynthia they were told that she worked there but had not come in to work and had not contacted anyone. This was very unusual for her. After again showing their badges, they asked to be taken to her office. The receptionist pressed a button and a young girl came from another room. She was told to take them to Cynthia's office on the 10th floor. While on the elevator Taylor questioned the girl but she had no knowledge of Cynthia.

They walked down the hall of the 10th floor. It was furnished with antique furniture and lighting. It was an expensive atmosphere. They arrived at Cynthia's office and her receptionist met them and introduced herself as Meg. She sent the girl back down stairs. After telling Meg about the murder they asked to go through her things, promising to put everything back in order. Meg was very hesitant but was assured they were investigating Cynthia's death and had no interest in anything else. They looked for half an hour and found nothing unusual. A small picture of a man and woman sat on the corner of the desk. Taylor wandered if it was her parents. Hanley took the picture and gave Meg a receipt. They showed the sketch to her and she had no idea who he was. She had never seen him before. While telling Meg they were leaving, they also let her know they might be back. Arriving on the ground floor, they showed the sketch to everyone but no one knew him. They were getting a gut feeling that Jason nor Cynthia's job had anything to do with what had happened to her.

They were feeling hungry and tired. The day had been long and tiresome. They caught the next ferry home with the feeling that they had somehow failed although there did not seem to be anything else they could have done.

CHAPTER 7

Taylor came back the next morning with news. Margaret Mailer had called the precinct wanting her or Hanley to come see her. As tired as she was she went to the hotel. She knocked on the door and again waited for it to be opened. Stepping inside Martha let the door close and lock before ushering Taylor in. She pointed to a chair and asked her to sit down. For some reason, she was very agitated. She was tired of being away from home and her own bed, and demanded that she be taken home. Taylor tried to reason with her but finally gave in to her wishes. No way they could keep her there if she did not want to stay. She relieved the guard telling him to come by the station in the morning and sign out.

Gathering up all Martha's belongings, and taking a last minute glance around they left the room stopping in the lobby at the reception counter. After checking her out, the clerk asked to speak to Taylor alone. Leaving Martha standing in front of the counter, she followed him into the clerk's work room behind the counter where he handed her a copy of the charges for the room. Looking them over Taylor noticed oddities in the statement. Why had she charged meals for two and the clerk wanted her to know that Margaret had also been spending a lot of time in the lobby reading. He had seen a gentleman there and they had spoken briefly. Taylor thanked him for his help and signed the paper work. She folded the paper with the charges and put it into her wallet.

When they reached the apartments, Martha asked if they could stop at my apartment. Taylor just said that I was not home for a few days not wanting to give anything away about the bombing and she did not want to scare Martha any more than she already was. All seemed quiet and well in the building and upon arriving at Martha's apartment Taylor checked to be sure that nothing was out of place, even looking under the bed. After much apprehension Taylor said goodnight and left her after cautioning her not to open the door for anyone she did not know. Again she told her not to tell anyone where she had been or anything that was happening.

After reaching her car, she sat for quite a long time trying to piece together what the clerk had told her. Why had Martha ordered meals for two? Was it possible that the gentleman from the lobby was just there looking for someone else or maybe he mistakenly thought she was some one else or did she actually know him? It seemed odd that she had not mentioned this. Why did she want to hurry home to her apartment? Did Martha meet a gentleman friend while she was there or was it more sinister than that. Something was not right. More questions were coming up with very few answers. Maybe Taylor would question the other hotel clerks. She decided to wait until tomorrow morning after she discussed all this with Hanley before she questioned Martha.

I was being released this afternoon from the hospital. Everything had been done for me that could be done. I had been tested, poked and prodded until I felt like a Thanksgiving turkey. I was more than ready to go home. The doctor told me that I had a minor concussion and was told to go home and rest for a few days. I was very lucky that I was not laying in pieces all over the parking lot. I was willing to do as I was told, looking forward to home and deciding to be more on the cautious side from then on. I was thinking that I must have a very hard head but might not be lucky next time.

Taylor came to the hospital and picked me up. While she drove me home, she explained about Martha and what the hotel clerk had told her. I also was in disbelief and couldn't begin to guess at what it all meant. She had been cautioned not to speak to strangers. If she was so afraid why would she do this. Hanley was having Martha followed at all times. We would just have to be cautious and not let her know that we were alerted to anything. Just act natural and she might accidentally drop some information.

I went to my apartment and just wanted to rest but this was not going to happen right away. The first thing I had to do was telephone my insurance company and notify them about my car being bombed. I was put on hold while the insurance agent located me a rental vehicle. The Ford dealership would have a rental car waiting for me but it would not be fancy. I figured my insurance rates would go sky high.

Calling a taxi was a better idea than to have someone in the building take me although a few had offered. I was not keen about going myself and I certainly did not want to put anyone else at risk. A salesman came out immediately. After I explained to him who I was, he took me inside the garage and showed me a two year old blue Ford. It had nothing special on it and it did not stand out in any way. Donavon signed the paper work, took the keys, started the car and left for home.

Sitting in his big chair was very relaxing. My last thoughts were to fix myself something to eat before I fell asleep. I woke up almost two hours later and was very hungry. I had finished eating and decided to take my coffee into the office and work for a couple hours and then go see Martha. With a jolt, a thought suddenly came to me. Finding Martha's file in the cabinet and taking it to my desk and opening it, I started to read. I pulled Cynthia's file and compared the dates. Martha had moved in to her apartment ten days after Cynthia had moved in. Her name was Martha Mailer born and raised in Chicago. She had retired from being a stewardess with American Airlines and was now on a pension. Having never married she left a sister's name and phone number as an emergency contact. Gathering my thoughts, I telephoned Taylor. After letting her know what I found out they both agreed that things were looking a lot more than just a coincidence. She took down all the information and said she would check it out.

Right now I just needed to think of other things. An hour later I had not accomplished a thing. My mind was kept busy with Martha. Grabbing my jacket I went up the stairs at a run. I would be happy when the crime tape was taken down and the elevator was again accessible. I will talk to Hanley about it.

While knocking on her door, I listened for any sound that might come from inside. When there was no response I knocked again. This time I heard the deadbolt slide back and the key in the door. Martha stood in the doorway making small talk as she invited me in. I listened to her explanation about coming home. She had not changed in any way, nor did she act any differently. It was possible she just wanted to come home but things were not really adding up that way. I decided to tell her about the car bombing and what I had been through. The television, radio and newspaper headlines would be screaming about it. She acted genuinely surprised and could hardly believe it. If she was involved with others, she had not been told about this. Nobody could fake the amazement or the fear in her eyes. After much discussion, I decided that she did not know about the bombing. I smiled gave her a hug and let her know that I would be home recuperating if she thought of anything.

CHAPTER 8

Standing at the window overlooking the garden was one of my favorite places to be other than in the garden itself. I was able to think calmly. Working with the plants and dirt was so peaceful and my favorite place to be. Looking out over the garden I could see it needed work. As soon as this case was solved and the security work complete, I will concentrate on getting it looking up to its potential. Some flowers needed to be cut back and the brown dead ones removed making room for new blooms. The work could keep me busy for weeks. Always something needed to be done and I enjoyed every bit of it.

The outside security camera at the store had caught the explosion but did not show anyone tampering with my car. Had the bomb been planted in my vehicle at another location. Maybe at the hotel or the carport in back of the apartments. Neither seemed likely but I would check them out.

I went out back to the carports and starting at one end going completely through them all. Finding nothing out of place I concluded that my car was not tampered with there. If it had been someone had cleaned the area well leaving nothing out of place. I had Security lights installed over each one earlier in the year and now I would have security cameras installed at different spots as soon as possible.

Getting into the rental car and checking everything out carefully, I drove to the hotel. I decided to check out the area that I parked in although it was probably futile. It looked just as a parking lot should look with asphalt and white parking lines. Going inside to reception, I rang the little bell on the counter. Soon a lady appeared to help me. After explaining why I was there, the lady became very helpful. She went to her files and came back, laying them open on the counter. Looking them over carefully it was concluded that no one had made any complaints about anything out of the ordinary. Not at the hotel or the parking lot. She took down my phone number and promised to call if she heard anything.

Going back to the store, I drove to the exact spot I had parked before. I knew the bomb had to have been rigged here. I sat and thought about how this could have been done. I walked around the car looking at the parking spots surrounding my car figuring a way it could have happened. A car was parked behind mine and one in front. A car parked beside me on the right side and a car came in beside me on the left side. One of the side cars could have faked problems with the hood opened. These vehicles could have been staged. While everyone was concentrating on the broken down vehicle, someone quickly planted the bomb. I remember seeing a car with the hood up but I thought no more about it. Nothing to do now but go on home and wait. Someone was working very hard to get rid of me. I must know something or have seen something but I do not have a clue to what it is.

The purse, wallet, laptop, jewelry and gloves had all been checked over in the lab. The only prints they could find were Todd's and Ron's from the pawn shop. These were only on the laptop and jewelry. The other prints were wiped clean on the purse and wallet. Things were at a standstill unless something else came up. The items were put in police storage until they were again needed. The question that kept coming back to me was if this was a robbery why did he throw everything away in the dumpster and who was the man that threw them there? Where is he and who is he? They had to get a break soon. It was certain that this had been staged to look like a robbery. Did someone dress Cynthia to look like she was going out? Why was she placed on our landing? Someone was going to great lengths, trouble and expense to throw the police off the scent.

It was a chilling thought to know that someone could come and go as they pleased throughout the building with nobody the wiser. I will be putting security locks on all entry ways and exits starting as soon as possible. Thinking that this was as good as time as any, I sat down at the phone and ordered security locks and cameras for the front of the building and the carport area. I was promised that the order would be sent to me as soon as possible.

I called Hanley but he was out of the office so I left him a message to call back. The residents wanted the crime tape removed so they could use the elevator. They had been very patient with all of this and now they were getting restless although they too wanted the crime solved. They had grown fond of Cynthia and missed her. They were afraid of the unknown and cautiously came and went.

When Hanley called back, I explained about the elevator. It was a real nuisance and inconvenience. I was told to take down the crime tape everywhere except around the apartment door. The detectives were not finished going through the apartment.

Suddenly everything came to life. The residents were happy and life was back to normal for them. The murder was on their minds but now other things were taking place and talked about. I had not realized just how quiet it was until the elevator started up with its metal against metal sounds. The eerie feeling that hung over the area was gone. The sound I learned to dislike was now welcomed. I called my carpet cleaning service explaining the problem and they came, cleaned and went. Everything had been cleaned up including the blood at the crime scene.

All building supplies came the next morning and I got started installing the security cameras. This would take most of the day. The security locks would be a different matter. I had hired the Ajax Lock Company to do the necessary work. To activate the locks would be something different. Each apartment would be given a card resembling a credit card for each tenant residing there whose name was on the lease. Once it was swiped in the slot beside the lock on the outer door the tenant would then enter the lobby, Here he would push a letter key and apartment number key embedded in the steel control panel on the wall.

A visitor could push a numbered button and be able to talk to and be seen by the corresponding numbered apartment. The person in the apartment could then push a button and open the outside door. This was a fairly simple, tried and true way to go. Having keys involved, could have a lot of problems. They could be lost or stolen making re-keying a costly, common procedure and it was very unsafe. This method was costing a lot of money but I know I want everyone safe including myself. The tenants would like and appreciate the things I have done.

I needed a break so I went in and fixed something to eat. Sitting at the table I could think only of the murder. Suddenly I remembered the pictures of the crime scene that I had taken and they were still in the camera. I have been so busy that I had forgotten about them. Jumping up, I got my camera off the desk and plugged it into the computer. I was soon looking at the pictures on the monitor. I hurried through all of the photos until I got to the crime scene photos.

There they were plain as day; pictures of Cynthia at different angles from a distance and up close. After setting up the printer with the right paper, I printed out two copies of each crime scene photo. One photo was different. I picked it up and discovered an image of someone looking around the corner of the crime scene. There was something familiar about this someone but I could not figure it out. I studied the image trying to think who it might be. This matter was up to Taylor to help with. Maybe with the modern equipment at their finger tips they could see the photo better and maybe find out who was in the photo.

I called Taylor and told her what my theory was on the car bombing. She thought it made a lot of sense. Then I told her about the photos. Taylor told me to come right in to the station and she would be waiting for me. Finding her at her desk I settled into a chair and we talked about the weather for a couple minutes. Then I handed her an envelope with the photos. She spread them around on the desk top. I pointed out the one with the image. It became a topic of importance. Several cops gathered around to take a look, but it was to hard to see anything.

Taylor picked up the phone and let the lab know she was on her way to see them. She took the envelope of photos and left. I knew I was not allowed to go to the lab but I would like to. I was assured that I would be the first to know if they found anything out. There was no reason that I should stay around so with that I left much more cautiously than I had been. Was this the reason someone was trying to kill me? Someone thinks I know more than I do. I will have to wait and see.

(HAPTER 9

As soon as I put the key in the lock I knew something was wrong. The door was unlocked and I opened it easily by pushing. Reaching around the door jamb, I felt for the living room light switch but someone grabbed my arm pulling me inside. I fought like a crazy person trying to get a hold on the guy to keep him from leaving. We fought through the living room into the kitchen where I was able to reach the kitchen light switch. The light came on and a rough looking bearded guy that I had never seen before took a swing at my jaw. I ducked to the side grabbing the other guy in a bear hug. As I released him I swung at his jaw putting all my weight behind it. The intruder became helplessly quiet. I threw him into a kitchen chair while I grabbed a length of rope that was lying with my garden things. After I tied the guys arms to the back of the chair I called Taylor.

I looked around at the mess we had made. My head started hurting again and my shoulders felt like lead pipes. I wished people would quit hitting me. The next time it happened I will hurt somebody bad. I took a look around while keeping an eye on the intruder. The glass top from my coffee table had been shattered and glass was all over the furniture and the floors. I picked up some of the broken pieces and put them into a garbage bag. The cushions were tossed about and books were dumped onto the floor when the book case was knocked over. Putting the garbage bag aside, I waited to straighten up the mess. The guy was coming around so I pulled a chair up close to him. I asked his name but there was no answer. I asked what he was doing here but again no answer. No matter what, I was not going to get any answers from this guy.

The doorbell began ringing and I opened the door for Taylor and Hanley pointing to the kitchen and they followed. They started asking all different questions, but they too were unsuccessful at getting answers. While Hanley threatened and tried to force him to answer, Taylor and I checked the apartment to see if anything was missing.

A few minutes later the detectives had the intruder in handcuffs. Before they left with him for the jail, they called the finger printing team in. Prints were taken from the doors knowing the intruder had to have touched them and dresser drawers in case he had gone though them. At the door as the three people were ready to leave, they noticed a crowd had gathered. Some of the neighbors had heard the ruckus and came to see what was happening. One guy stood out from the rest and did not belong in the apartments. I yelled at him as Hanley gave chase but the stranger ran for the lobby and disappeared. No one seemed to know who he was. At least they were keeping quiet not wanting to get involved.

Taylor wanted to run the guy's description right away. The guy was about forty years old, with a surly attitude and a two inch scar on the right side of his head. He was about six foot, around one hundred and seventy five pounds, with short blond hair, wearing a faded Seahawks shirt and blue jeans with brown construction boots. He was a rough looking guy and could have been off a fishing boat in Seattle. Maybe his description with the scar would help identify the guy. He had not committed a crime that we knew of but he might know something. He seemed to be too interested in events. This guy fit the description of the sketch of the guy at the dumpster given by Todd Warren. There was just enough difference to make a person wonder if the guy today was disguised. Maybe something would open up for them.

I was hurting real bad and took some aspirins and I sat down among the mess in my big chair and rested. The cleanup could wait. One thing for sure I will hurry up the work on the new security cameras. The security people would start work in the morning.

I woke up the next morning with a headache and I was very stiff and sore. Very reluctant and wanting to roll over and go back to sleep, I did manage to get out of bed and make coffee. Looking out the window I could see a clear sky and a beautiful sunny day. Working in the garden would be very relaxing and thinking of something other than the case would be nice. I was busy pulling weeds down on my knees when Taylor came up to me.

The intruder in the apartment was a transient by the name of Berry Ross. He had been hired and paid by an elderly lady fitting Martha's description to go into my apartment to find and steal the photos of the crime scene. He told the detectives he was broke and needed the money or he would not have done it. Nothing could be found as far as a rap sheet went. He must have been a first time offender, like he said. He was turned over to guards and led off to jail. It was a common thought among all that he had nothing to do with anything other than breaking and entering and being stupid.

Martha was next to be visited as far as I was concerned. I am not ready to reveal all to her but I will just check on her and talk about the crime but not leave clues for her. Maybe she will make a mistake and let some thing slip. I will do this as soon as possible. It seemed to be an immediate problem and things were starting to come together. How was she involved in all of this?

The lab was able to get a much clearer image of the guy at the crime scene. Taylor had called me to come to the station and see what had been found. She handed the photo to me and asked me to take a look. Maybe I would recognize him or it might jolt a memory. I did recognize him but from where I could not remember. Suddenly it dawned on me as I gave the photo back to Taylor and told her to study it very closely. I was sure she would find him familiar. She knew what I meant. The guy in the photo was the same guy that had thrown Cynthia's belongings in the dumpster. It was agreed that the sketch of the guy from the dumpster, the guy in the crowd at the apartment and the guy in the photo was the same person. Now to find out who this guy is. Taylor called her chief at the precinct and relayed all the information they had collected. The chief immediately put out an all points bulletin on the guy using all three pictures. Hopefully it would not be long before they heard something.

I had sent for two tickets to a Mariners' game before all this happened. I always buy two and then would ask one of the tenants to go along. I thought it would be nice to ask Taylor to go. I think she would be fun to be with. She thought it would be fun to go. We both need a day away from everything. I was jittery and nervous like a school boy. She told me that she was a widow of a police sergeant with two grown married girls and grandchildren. I had never married or even gotten engaged. The job always seemed to get in the way of anything permanent. I had been married to my work.

CHAPTER 10

Loading ourselves down with hot dogs and sodas we were then escorted to our aisle seats three rows back between home plate and the first base line giving us the ability to see all that was happening. The weather was co-operating with blue skies and eighty degrees making it possible to open the retractable roof. Soon the game was underway with the Texas Rangers up first. Three batters came up and three batters went down. The Mariners came up and it seemed to go the same way with three batters up and three batters down. The score remained zero to zero until Griffey hit a home run in the third and brought two runners home. The crowd went wild with their cheering and the 'wave' started. The excitement was growing. In the fifth inning the Rangers got three runs tying the score three to three. The score remained tied taking the game into the tenth inning. Martinez was up and the crowd went crazy. Standing first on one foot then the other and putting his hands just right on the bat he was ready. The pitcher threw a curve ball perfectly right down the middle, Martinez swung, slamming a homer into center field ending the game. The stadium seemed to explode. People were cheering and shouting all the way out to the exit. I was attempting to keep a watch on the crowds as much as possible for anyone more concerned with Amy or me.

We had a great time and decided to do something together again soon. We stopped at Ivars By the Sea ordering seafood dinners and wine. We talked and ate thoroughly enjoying each others company and touching on the crime and what was happening, and hoping that it would soon be over. She talked about her children and grandchildren. The time seemed to fly by much too fast, it was time to catch the ferry for home. We were both sorry to see the evening end. I drove Amy home walking her to her door shyly hugging her and gave her a big kiss. She hugged me and kissed me back showing that she really liked me and wanted to get together soon. I knew that I was falling in love fast and had never felt like this before. I watched as she went inside and turned the lights on. She was a very attractive brunette around one hundred thirty pounds probably in her late forties or early fifties. To me she was gorgeous and I would definitely be seeing more of her.

Arriving home nothing seemed out of place. Routinely, I took a look around before I went into my apartment. Automatically turning on the television to get the evening news after I grabbed a beer from the refrigerator I settled into my big chair to watch.

There was some minor news and suddenly a special news break came on the air. An all points bulletin came on with the three pictures of the mystery man. I hurried out of the chair and turned the volume up. The Newscaster was explaining about the pictures and the belief they were of the same man. At the same time she was giving a description of each picture. She told the viewers that he was wanted for questioning in connection with the murder of Sandra Roma A.K.A. Cynthia Marquet. A small amount was told about the murder scene and the Majestic Apartments. The viewers were cautioned not to talk to or approach this man in any way. He was believed to be armed and dangerous. If any one knew anything please contact the Bremington Police and ask for Detective Hanley or Detective Taylor. Again they were cautioned not to approach this man in any way.

First thing the next morning, I received a call from Amy thanking me for the Mariners game and the dinner. She had a wonderful time thoroughly enjoying the evening. Letting her know that I was looking forward to doing something else with her, I asked her to come up with something she would like to do. We discussed the newscast. So far no one had come forward but it was still early and the nature of people was to double guess themselves before they could make a decision. It was dangerous and most people were public minded but not very courageous.

I told her of my plans to see Martha and see if maybe I could find something out without asking questions. She agreed saying it was better for me to do it than her. I could be casual and nonchalant. She might give something away. Who would have thought that this nice little lady could be involved with such a mess as this?

First I would need to get groceries. I had not gotten many only enough to get by with from the store two blocks away. Just as I was getting into the car and driving away, I thought I heard a gun shot. Looking around and seeing nothing was wrong I decided I was getting paranoid. When suddenly a shot rang out and blew out the rear window of my car, just missing my ear. Speeding up all the while looking around I saw a newer light green Chevrolet Malibu in my rear view mirror, with a guy hanging out the window with a rifle shooting at me. With tires screeching, I made a fast turn out of the alley into traffic. I hoped my followers would at least slow down but it was not happening. I continued traveling at a high speed, watching the blocks go by and dodging the cars. I hoped I would be stopped by a cop but none were to be seen. Realizing I was close to the police station, I hit the brakes turning the wheel at the same time, skidding to the front of the building. I jumped from the car keeping my head down as I moved past each patrol car reaching the door just as the green Chevrolet slowed down and drove past me making it easy to get the license number.

I went straight to Taylor's office where she and Hanley were up to their elbows in paper work. Both were very surprised to see me. When they realized I was shaken up and something was wrong both started asking me questions. I poured myself a cup of coffee and pulled up a chair while explaining what had just happened. An all points bulletin was put out immediately on the green Chevrolet. They were sure that it was stolen and would soon be found. It would then be towed into the evidence yard and gone over for finger prints or any other evidence that could be found.

The blue Ford Fusion would also be towed into the evidence yard. I would need to put in a call to the Ford dealership explaining the situation and give my insurance agent another call. It seemed like a good decision not to get another vehicle until this case was solved. Getting around could get to be a real problem but for now Amy offered to take me home and we would check things out there. She asked me questions knowing there were no answers. Their Police Captain was pushing them to work harder. He also suggested a cop be with me until this was resolved but I refused. Everyone was working as fast as possible to find answers and solve this murder. Nothing had come in since the news bulletin but as soon as the people realized anything they might know, they would soon be calling. In the mean time I would see Martha. This had become a crucial thing to do and I could not wait around for things to happen.

I had asked to stop by the grocery store on the way home. Amy was driving her own vehicle, a newer black vehicle, as a patrol car would stand out. Shopping should not take us long. I had my list of things I needed in my pocket. She took part of the list to hurry things along. Neither of us felt comfortable in the store after all that had happened. As the clerk checked us out my attention was on the people in the store. No one looked out of place or suspicious and so I paid, and we went out the door headed for the car and home.

CHAPTER 11

Digging in the wet dirt and planting flowers was very relaxing and gave me a feeling of accomplishment. I was busy cutting away the dead flowers and leaves making the garden look like new, while the vibrant colors and aromas took my breath away. My concentration and thoughts were on the garden forgetting all time. Looking at my watch I saw it was four thirty. I had been working since breakfast and was feeling hungry so putting the tools away I called it a day. Maybe tomorrow I would be able to come and enjoy the garden some more.

I was getting things from the cabinet to fix supper when the house phone rang. Answering it was a must. The caller was not giving up and the phone rang steadily. Empting my hands I picked up the telephone and heard Taylor ask me where I had been. She had tried to call me all day on both phones and was worried and upset. If I had not answered she would have come to my apartment. With things the way they were I was not being very smart by not checking in with her. Without thinking

I had left my cell phone on the kitchen table. The day had been relaxing but I was upset at myself for not calling her. There was no excuse and she did not deserve to have to worry all day. I explained, apologized and asked her to dinner. She accepted but was still hurt by my inconsideration. Telling her that I would be ready in an hour she agreed to pick me up.

As she honked the horn she saw someone in the garden. Thinking it was me she hollered just as I came out the door. Pointing at the garden she jumped from the car and gave chase, going cautiously along the wall. Seeing where she was I went along the opposite side staying close to the wall. We kept watch over the garden so he did not double back and get away. A mans figure sprang up, looming into sight as he attempted to climb the high sheer stone fence at the back of the garden. He seemed to have found a good toe hold in the fence just as Amy came up behind and grabbed him from the back by the shoulder and arm dragging him from the fence onto the ground where she quickly handcuffed him before he could react. I came running to them with gun in hand and seeing that the situation was under control I holstered my weapon.

Seeing the intruder and recognizing him was a surprise. The man that had an all points bulletin out looking for him. The person of many disguises was right in front of us. What was he doing here? Did he come to see Martha or was it more sinister than that? It had to be something of importance for him to take such a chance as this.

As Taylor put the man in the back seat of her car she told him his rights. I climbed in beside him again pulling out my gun, and I kept it pointed at the intruder making sure he did not get away again. Taylor began asking him questions but was getting nowhere. This guy had a lot to answer for. Did he murder Sandra? If so, how and why? Did someone pay him to do this? Did he work for the mob or Jack Roma? Did he know Martha Mailer if so from where? Were they working together? The answers would come but how long it would take was another mystery.

Dinner would have to wait for another night. After taking the guy to the police station where he was finger printed, hours were spent attempting to extract information from him. He became very surly and belligerent as he was questioned. Hanley told him that there was a witness at the dumpster scene where he was seen throwing away Sandra's laptop and jewelry. He had been seen at the Majestic Apartments in the crowd by me and his image appeared in a photo of the crime scene showing him standing in the background.

He began to show nervousness as he considered the evidence against him. He asked for a lawyer and then remained quiet. Hanley left the interrogation room as soon as an attorney came in. He was not going to do anything that would cause this thug to go free.

Since no one was able to get the man's name, Taylor sat down at the computer and put his three pictures and finger prints onto the FBI and Criminal lists. They had ran through thousands of photos when the machine started making noises to show that his photo was found. Name is Harry Belmont, age forty-seven, born in Seattle, WA. Alias, Norman Greene, Marty Crenshaw, Pete Wright. He had been in trouble most of his adult life. She gave herself a lecture on waiting for backup and at least waiting for me. This guy was very dangerous and she could have gotten badly hurt but she did not want him to escape. She decided that she had done the right thing. Finding the captain in his office, she asked him to notify the media.

While she did a report on Belmont's capture, I stretched out on the couch in the captains office. I was starting to feel better but not up to a hundred percent. The television was on and I was not watching anything special. My mind was on the crime and of course Amy when the TV station again interrupted with breaking news. The three pictures were again shown with the arrest photo using Belmont's real name and his aliases. If anyone knew anything about this person please notify the Bremington police and ask for Detective Taylor or Detective Hanley. The newscaster was telling about the capture and the part that Detective Taylor had played in all of this. She was given a hero's yell in the squad room. They tried to bring up my part of the capture, but I wanted nothing to do with any of it. Let her be the hero. She was very deserving of all the glory never giving thought to the danger to herself, only arresting the guy and getting the information. She was a great detective and public servant.

Amy received a phone call from the jail. Belmont was wanting to talk to her. The guard wanted him to wait, but he insisted it be now. A cop accompanied her and they went off to the jail. Belmont was waiting at a table in the interrogation room. Amy asked him why the change of heart. He told her that he was more afraid of what Jack could do even if he were in jail, than of her or even prison. What he did know was he wanted Jack to take the fall too.

Amy asked him how he was involved. Belmont told her this story. Jack heard about me at a tuna cannery in Seattle. I had done some jobs that others would not do. Nothing like this. Jack had paid me fifty thousand dollars to kill his niece. I went to her apartment, dressed in fancy clothes and met Jack there. The lady was knocked out and slumped over the arm of a large sofa. I was told to take her and place her like you seen her, in the fancy clothes so that the police would think it was from outside. After I had her arranged and using my air gun I shot her just behind the ear. I was looking for the small wooden pea I had used when I heard somebody coming. Backing up as far as I could so not to be seen, I was thinking I was safe until the manager started taking pictures. I watched for him to leave and then took the jewelry, the laptop, wallet and purse that I had hidden in my coat and I tossed them into the dumpster. Making the murder look like robbery.

Still thinking that I was okay, I would return later around dinner time in my everyday clothes. Everyone would be eating at this time and I could look for the pea. As I came up the steps I saw the manager looking over the crime scene, moving small pieces of wood around. I was able to get behind the guy and lay him out with the butt of my pistol. I only looked for a minute and left.

He told Amy that he had gone back but something was happening in the managers apartment and he wanted to see what. Someone pointed and yelled at him and he fled.

Tonight he took another chance and went back again. He figured if the pea could not be found there would be no murder weapon. As he was going around the hedge, the manager opened the door, so he turned to hide, but Amy showed up catching him in the car head lights. You know the rest.

Hanley wanted to know what was so special about the wooden pea. The answer was that he made them special, from a special wood from South America. A lot of different people knew this and would remember. It was like a signature. He was calling Roma a coward among all the other things as he was led back to jail. He was ready to go to court.

CHAPTER 12

Amy invited me for coffee at her house before taking me home. We spent an easy two hours talking about police work and different cases each of us had been involved with over the years. One of her cases had involved a serial killer. She was very graphic in her telling of the things he had done and the people he had killed. The whole thing had gotten to her and she had given a lot of thought to giving up police work altogether. Her family had convinced her to take some time off and think about everything. Knowing the department was her life she went back to work and was able to work through the depression, glad that she had listened. Once in a while the case would come back and disturb her but it was much easier now to deal with.

She mentioned that Todd Warren would get a phone call after the trials were ended. No one had come forward to claim the jewelry, laptop, wallet and purse. Hopefully he could sell them and put the money to good use. He now knew what the money value was for each piece.

The subject of Amy's family came up and she brought out many pictures of her kids and grandkids explaining who each one was. The older daughter Beth was married to Derek Parks and has two boys Pete and Gary, ages six and four years old. Carol the younger daughter was married to Pat Lange and has a three year old boy, Mike. The family was very close and were always there for each other. I started thinking of my life having very little meaning since I had retired from the police force. I was an only child, both of my parents had died when I was younger. All my relatives were in Iowa and I had not heard from them in many years. When I was given the opportunity to partner up in the apartments with a Real Estate broker, I made them my life just this minute I realized what I had missed out on. It would be wonderful being part of Amy's family and life. What would my attributes be? I was not the handsomest man around but I was not bad looking either. With having a very good pension, money in the bank, and a good income I knew that money would not be a problem. I would be close to home if some problem should arise and I would always be there for her and the family. Besides all of this we had our careers in common.

Someday, I will ask her to marry me and hope I am not rushing things. We have only known each other a short time, but I am hoping she will say yes. How would her family react to this? I will hint at her having a barbecue or some family get together. If all goes well and I am accepted, I will get an

on with her pretense saying that the gentleman was from out of town, Chicago she thought, and did not know anyone. She felt sorry for him and invited him for dinner. The man had said he would be back in town soon and would come and see her. Continuing on with her act she told me that she hoped it was okay with the detectives that she had invited him. I asked her if everything was okay with her and she replied that it was. Standing up I gave her a hug so she would not think something was amiss.

My mind really started working big time. She admitted to me that she had dinner in her room at the motel with a gentleman from Chicago and that he would be returning. After she had been cautioned not to, she must have given him her phone number and or address. She did not act as though I was any kind of threat to her. I am sure that she had not been told anything about the investigation and hoped she would not hear from Jack until we had more time with the people in jail. This would probably be my last visit before she was taken into custody.

Amy stopped by to see if I needed anything. I gave her a kiss and then we went to the kitchen and had coffee and talked. I told her about Martha and the man from Chicago. Figuring she was lying again, we figured he was from New York not Chicago. Was this Jack Roma? What is their connection? Amy called the precinct and talked to Hanley and asked him to get an okay for a plain clothed police officer to shadow Martha around the clock. She hoped to catch the man and Martha together. In the mean time she would run a check on Martha Mailer to find out who she really is. It seemed doubtful that she told the truth about this.

Returning to the station she put Martha's picture on the police list on the computer. Amy was really surprised when it came back as Martha Murphy age fifty-nine, born in Chicago, IL. Airline stewardess American Air Lines. Retired. She called me as soon as it came back. They had enough circumstantial evidence to pick her up. They decided to wait and maybe one of these guys would give her up, strengthening the case against her. All I could think of was what a mess. How did she get involved in something like this?

Things were starting to get interesting as far as the investigation was going. The green Chevrolet Malibu was found abandoned at Evergreen Park by the water. The police had completely gone through it from the hood to the trunk. One set of prints came up several times and they were put in the computer. They came up belonging to a small time hood by the name of Cab Nelson. He was being picked up and brought in for questioning. The vehicle had been stolen from the college parking lot and belonged to a student. After the police were finished with it, the car was returned to the owner.

I was asked to go with Amy back to the precinct while her and Hanley interrogated Cab Nelson. Without hesitation I grabbed my jacket and cap, and opened the door for her. In a matter of a few minutes we were on our way downtown. Finally we were coming up with something to go on. Who had hired this guy and his buddies? Hopefully all of them could be brought in and jailed soon.

Cab denied having anything to do with the Malibu and kept claiming that we made a mistake or we were trying to frame him. When asked where he was at the time of the shooting his alibi was that he was playing pool at Boyd's Bar. He did admit to having friends around but he was sure they were not involved either. Hanley showed him a picture of Martha and also a picture of Belmont telling him that these people were connected and what did he know about them? This information caused him to shut down except to ask for an attorney. Amy told him that he and his pals would be facing attempted murder charges.

A rather nervous, not-too-smart guy came to the jail looking for Cab claiming to be his brother. Hanley immediately took him in for questioning. He said that his name was Russ and that Cab was his older brother. When asked where he was the day of the shooting, he said that he and Cab were at the movies. Amy told him what Cab had said about playing pool. Russ became very nervous at this point and said we could ask Kip and Jer, friends that had gone to the movies with them.

Leaving Hanley to question Russ, Amy talked to two cops in the station and told them to go to Boyd's Bar and see if they could find kip and Jer and bring them in for questioning. Hopefully the police would have the gang that bombed my car and shot up the blue Ford rental car. We could at least find out who paid them. Going back to Russ, she showed him Martha and Belmont's pictures and asked him if he had ever seen either of them before. He denied knowing anything. Cab and whoever was with him would be charged with attempted murder and grand theft auto. Amy had to find a way to tie Russ, Kip and Jer in with Cab. The police had to come up with proof or find a way to get one of them talking.

Hanley and Amy left the room giving Russ time to think about all he was told. Cab was in one room while Russ was in another. The detectives thought it might be a good idea to put them in the same room to see what would happen. Russ was taken to Cab's room and left there. The brothers were not aware the room had microphones and cameras in each corner.

Watching through the window with mirror glass and listening to the conversation between the brothers got interesting. They just looked at each other for a minute before Cab asked what he was doing there? Russ explained that Jer had called saying that he was with Cab when he was picked up and he told me to come bail my brother out. As soon as he arrived he was brought in for questioning. Cab wanted to know what he had told the cops. Russ told him about being at the movies because that was his first thought. Cab started to yell at him and told him how dumb he was. He told him to tell the cops that he had lied and that they were really playing pool but not to mention Jer or Kip. Russ was afraid to tell him that he already had. Cab could be real mean when he was angry. Russ was not to mention the Malibu or anything to do with it. They clammed up and just sat staring at each other.

Hanley and Taylor opened the door to the interrogation room. Hanley told them they were under arrest for attempted murder, grand theft auto, weapon charges, public endangerment and anything else that would come up. They would be in prison for along time. Was there anything they would like to talk about to make it easier on themselves. The brothers were immediately handcuffed, read their legal rights. They were taken off to jail by two cops. Cab was loudly cussing and accusing Russ of telling the cops everything. They were both yelling for an attorney. Amy was glad they had two of the bunch and waited for the other two to be brought in.

CHAPTER 13

I awoke to a beautiful day with the sun shinning, not a cloud to be seen, and there was a light warm breeze. Today I will spend the day working in the garden. Maybe do some planting and finishing up what I had started. Nothing was happening at this point in the case concerning me. Working would occupy my time while I waited to hear from Amy. Sticking my cell phone into my pocket, I headed to the garden. The wonderful scents of the flowers met me and I had a feeling of warmth and nostalgia from my childhood and my mother's garden.

Amy called at one o'clock to let me know the police had picked up Jer and Kip at Boyd's Bar. They began by denying knowing anything about what Cab had done and also said they did not know much about Cab or his brother. They were always around the bar shooting pool or chewing the fat with the guys. A person could tell that their story was well rehearsed. Each guy told the same story almost word for word. Because it was easier to get information from Russ, he was brought in to identify the two. Standing in front of the same mirrored room, where Jer and Kip were sitting, Amy asked Russ to tell her the names of the guys in the room. He made them promise that they would not tell Cab. He told them that the skinny guy was Jer and the stocky guy was Kip but did not know their last names. When he was asked where he knew them from Russ said they had been friends of his brother for years and they hung around Boyd's Bar a lot.

Again entering the room, Amy approached Jer and Kip. She asked if they wanted to change their story in any way. She informed them that Russ had identified them as long time friends of Cab's. Bringing up the attempted murder charges, grand theft auto, weapon charges, public endangerment and what else might come up to charge them with. She informed them that Cab nor Russ would take the rap alone so they might save themselves some trouble by coming clean. Neither of them answered her. They were read their rights then taken to the jail where they would be given the afternoon to think about everything. Hanley would try to get a confession from one of the four later in the day. She did not think it would be long before each one of them realized that one of the others would rat them out.

I listened with great anticipation to what Amy was saying. I also felt that it would not be long before one of the gang gave it all up blaming the others. I knew that Martha would be brought into it and charged with all the crimes including the murder of Cynthia. Knowing that they all would spend their lives in prison was great news to me. They would have to pay for their crimes and then Sandra Roma would be at peace.

I returned to the garden work with much vigor. With the case starting to come together I could relax and concentrate on the weeds. What a great day it was. My phone rang interrupting my thoughts. I was surprised when Robert Devon answered my hello. No one had heard from him since the bombing. So much had happened since we last talked. He asked me for news and as before I referred him to the detectives. His explanation was that he was busy on another case and knew he was not needed here so he left everything to the detectives. They seemed very thorough and on top of things. If he was needed he could be contacted. Before we hung up he let me know that he would check in with Hanley or Taylor.

I have had a bad feeling about Devon ever since my car was bombed. The feeling kept creeping into my thoughts. This time I could not talk myself out of it or push the thoughts away. I called Amy and told her. We decided that maybe we should be more careful where he was concerned and not so forthcoming with information. I learned years ago that a gut feeling was usually right so I held to it.

I studied in my mind what we knew about Robert Devon. Was he really on the up and up or had he turned bad? He and his partner showed up first when Sandra was at the airport leaving Florida for Alaska. At this time Devon told her that her father had made a deal with the FBI. In return for telling all he knew about the mafia, the FBI would protect and keep his daughter safe. He next showed up in Alaska when her friend was beaten and at which time she left Alaska for Honolulu, Hawaii. Why did he give Sandra a card? Was it so he could keep track of her or because Jack paid him too. Why was he really at the store when my car was blown up? Just what is his involvement in all of this? Have we trusted him to much?. Things were not coming together with any clarity, just suspicion of a guy we are suppose to be able to trust. I was getting too many questions without answers causing me to be more confused.

At some time the detectives would need to ask him to come in for a few questions. They had to have a solid reason or the FBI would come down hard on them. They can handle this I am sure. One way or another his part in all of this will come to light.

A police informant notified Hanley that word on the street was that a guy fitting Jack Roma's description was hanging around Boyd's Bar. He just seemed to show up out of nowhere. Two cops with police backup were sent to check out the information and to arrest him. When they got there Jack had vanished. The bartender was questioned and shown Jack's picture. He said that Jack had come in that day and played pool for a while and bought beer

CHAPTER 14

Amy had invited me to her house for a homemade dinner. I called a taxi to get there so I would not bother her while she cooked. I arrived an hour to soon but this was okay with her. She fixed us each a Martini and we sat and visited until the dinner was ready. I tried to help her by setting the table. I think I was more in the way than helpful but she did not complain. She told me it was nice for me to be there.

She was a great cook and had spent some time cooking a roast beef dinner with all the trimmings. She had spent the afternoon baking dinner rolls and a cherry pie. While we ate we talked about the case and her family. I told her that all the security work was finished at the apartments and I felt at ease by this. There would not be any more surprises without someone knowing about it.

I felt this was a good time to talk about a barbecue. She smiled at me with excitement in her voice, letting me know she thought this was a great idea. She would call her girls right away and set up a time. We agreed that Sunday was best. Taking me into her backyard she showed me her new brick barbecue. I was surprised at it's size, large enough to cook for a hundred people. This would be a good time to try it out. I offered to bring ribs and cook them with my special sauce and would bring anything else that was needed. She told me to just bring myself and the ribs, that her and the girls would handle the rest.

There was a large round table with an equally large umbrella to cover it. Several large evergreen trees here and there in no special order and a chain link fence surrounded the enormously large yard giving the area a sense of security and privacy. She had a lot of ideas on landscaping. When the girls were growing up, she worked and now that the girls were grown up with lives of their own she felt free to spend the time and money.

We went back into the kitchen. As she put the food away, I scraped and stacked the dirty dishes. She then washed them and I dried asking her every now and then where the items went. We both laughed and enjoyed each other.

We sat on the sofa and relaxed while I just held her. She was as content as I was. We attempted to watch a TV movie but I could not tell you what it was about. It was starting to get late so I suggested that she take me home. She turned towards me, putting her arms around me, gave me a big kiss and told me that she had not felt this way about anyone since her husband had died of a gunshot wound fifteen years earlier after being shot by a man high on drugs. I told her how I felt about her and we kissed. She stood up saying I was right, and it was time for us to go. She went into her bedroom, got her purse and we left.

Just as we pulled up in front of the apartments, we noticed a guy with a cap covering his face and wearing an overly large black jacket. He came from the apartments, showing no recognition as he headed down the street. We looked at each other thinking that it may be Jack in disguise. Amy called the station, giving the police details to have the guy followed. He probably was carrying a gun in his pocket so we were cautious. We got back into the car and drove down the street to see if we could get a glimpse of this person but he had turned at the corner and we went straight sending an all points bulletin out. At this time we learned that the undercover cop had notified the precinct only minutes before describing Jack. Suddenly we heard sirens and seen the patrol cars swarming around the area.

Jack ran, eluding the officers and dogs. He tried to hide in an old tumbled down shed but the dogs sniffed him out and he ran again. This time he climbed a ladder into a tree-house leaving himself no way out. The officers circled the trunk of the tree using shrubs and other places to hide until Jack started shooting at them. They shot back not wanting to kill him. They wanted him alive for the trial. Killing him would be to easy a way out.

He had to pay for his crimes. The Captain yelled at him several times to throw down his weapon and surrender but he choose to keep shooting. The air seemed to explode with Jack's scream as a bullet tore upward through his thigh. He yelled that he was surrendering as he threw his colt 38 away from him and it dropped to the ground below. Someone yelled cease fire and all the guns went silent. Two officers went up the ladder where Jack sat with his arms in the air and the blood running down his leg. One officer ran to his patrol car and grabbed the medical kit. An ambulance was called as the leg of his slacks was cut away and a tourniquet was put around the upper part of his leg. It seemed as though not much time had gone by when the EMT'S handed up a gurney to the officers and they followed up the ladder behind it. Jack was given a tetanus shot and the tourniquet was adjusted. He was then brought down out of the tree-house, put into the ambulance and sent to the emergency room at the hospital. There were three guards with him at all times in the ambulance and while he was transferred to the hospital where he was taken into surgery. Three guards were to be with him at all times even in the operating room. When all was finished he was taken to a private room and handcuffed to his bed. The Dr. suggested that he remain in the hospital for a few days.

Amy was off duty so we remained by her vehicle as the officers moved in on Jack. I mentioned that it was a good feeling to have the security at the apartments. Jack must have had Martha's help getting inside. They would then have to deal with the undercover cop who would be watching every move they made. It was very doubtful the man could have been a friend of another tenant with nothing sinister involved. If he were a friend he would have waved or spoken to us. As it were he was trying to get away without any exchange.

We watched while the cops went after Jack, running with their guns drawn and K-9 units. The patrol cars were circulating around the area. He would not get very far nor would he be able to hide among the large trees or buildings. Like a large welcoming boom we heard someone yelling that Jack was comprehended and in handcuffs.

Not waiting for Martha to get word of this, we turned toward the apartments, parked and went inside not stopping until we reached Martha's apartment. Amy stood at the side so she could not be seen while I knocked on the door. There was no answer so I rang her door bell. She came to the door, opening it and invited me in with a smile on her face. Amy stepped into the doorway following me inside. Martha's smile quickly turned to a look of alarm as she realized we had not come as friends. Amy read her rights to her as she put her in handcuffs. I opened the door leading the way to the elevator surprised that we had not seen a tenant.

Amy opened the door to the back seat of the car as she put Martha inside. I opened up the other door and slid inside beside her so I could keep watch. As we drove away, Amy asked her how she had gotten involved with Jack but she did not receive an answer. She was told that we had arrested everyone involved and Jack would probably be there when we arrived along with Robert Devon, who was brought in earlier for questioning. She would be questioned and booked on murder charges, attempted murder, Grand theft auto, along with anything else that came up.

The station was a loud and busy place. The cops were all around looking busy as they had been brought in to stand guard. Martha was seated at Amy's desk. Amy asked her if she wanted an attorney. She told us maybe later she would. Mug shots were taken, she was finger printed and then taken into an interrogation room.

Martha broke down crying. She was very scared and as she should be. She was in one bad mess. She told us that she had really liked Sandra and in a different circumstance she would have liked to have been friends. She went on to tell us that she knew Jack from her days working as a stewardess with the larger airline companies. He was a frequent flyer from New York City to all the larger cities around the country. They had been more than friends for many years. Going to the best parties, mingling with the idly rich, and meeting the upper crust. The people seemed to have a lot of respect for the guy but she only had a hint of what he really was. There had been talk of marriage a couple of times but nothing ever came of it.

He had never involved her in anything until now. She was asked by Jack to move into the apartments and find out what she could about Sandra. She found her to be a likeable person and befriended her. Sandra Roma had told her everything about her life and uncle Jack. Everything was reported to Jack. She had not realized that this would only be the start of what Jack wanted her to do until the night of Sandra's death. She was to invite herself for drinks at Sandra's apartment and put knock-out drops into Sandra's, drops he had given to her earlier. As soon as she passed out, Martha put on plastic gloves and went into her closet and brought out fancy evening clothes, changing Sandra into to these, hanging the other clothes carefully on the hangers in the closet so nothing looked out of place. She carefully washed the drink glasses and put them away in the cabinet. Jack arrived with Belmont and told Martha to go home. In her gut she knew something bad was going was going to happen but she chose to go to her apartment and lock the door. When she heard all about it after the police came, she acted as surprised and shocked as everyone else.

Martha tried to convince us that she did not want to do any of these things and told Jack so, thinking he would get someone else. In this brief instant she really discovered and got to know Jack for what and who he was. After that he threatened her into doing what he wanted. He told her to fake being afraid so she would be sent to a hotel or somewhere easier to see him without being in danger of being noticed. He came to dinner at the hotel to see her and at that time told her to go back to her apartment until he could finish his work and they could leave Bremington, which would not be very long. He contacted her again to meet him at the diner where he gave her an envelope with money in it and the name of Barry Ross. She met with this guy at the park and gave him the envelope. I never knew what it was for.

Amy asked her if she knew this guy had torn up my apartment and had a fist fight with me. Did she know what he was looking for? She of course denied knowing. Only that she had met the man and gave him the envelope.

Jack then called to have her meet him on the corner two blocks away from her apartment. He gave her another envelope with instructions. This time she was to go to Boyd's Bar and ask for a guy by the name of Cab. Give him the envelope with the instructions and then leave. She swore that is all she did.

Hanley asked her a couple questions. Had she thought about looking into the envelope and her answer was yes but she had not. She was afraid of what she would find out and she did not want to know. Did she know she had paid the hit man to blow up my car with me in it? She looked at him and said that she had not meant to kill anyone. She was just doing what Jack insisted that she do. Was Jack at her apartment tonight at any time and if so why? Her short answer was that he had come to be sure she kept her mouth shut and to get something to eat. She was so afraid of the man who had been the love of her life.

As Martha was being returned to her cell, she asked to speak to me. Amy came and got me from the captain's office. Martha told me that she really liked me and liked living at the apartments. She told how she had called me and that she was the voice. She wanted me to know right away about Sandra. The detectives would bring her back again for questioning after the others had been questioned. Tight security was put up every where just so Jack did not have any more surprises up his sleeve.

Hanley told Amy that she might as well go home. It was getting late and nothing more would be happening until morning when they hoped to question Jack. Arriving back at the apartments, Amy decided to come in with me to be sure all was as it should be. After checking everything out, I invited her to spend the night. After all we were grown-ups and did not have to answer to others. We had a drink to relax and sat talking for a long time about everything we knew. We made our way into the bedroom feeling we were in unfamiliar waters, very nervous and not at all sure of ourselves. Soon we were in bed and everything was alright from there. We held each other and kissed and made love into the night. I knew I loved her and she loved me. I knew that we were meant to be. I had to be the happiest guy around.

CHAPTER 15

Reading the newspaper and having my coffee each morning is a habit that I have had ever since I can remember. It starts the day out on the right note. The front page was full of the capture of Jack Roma and his paid gang. Their pictures were all on the front page. The trial was starting on Monday making it one week from now. Jack still was not saying anything. Amy and Hanley both had been to the hospital several times to talk to him. He would be released from the hospital on Sunday afternoon and transported to the jail. We were very sure he would be convicted of all charges. We had the confessions of all other parties involved. They all had been arraigned and waiting in jail for court day. John (Jack) Roma of New York City, and Martha Murphy of Chicago were being held on Murder charges, Attempted Murder charges, Weapon charges, Grand Theft Auto, and Public Endangerment charges. Each of his gang would be looking at the same charges. The judge was showing leniency at Barry Ross's arraignment. He felt he was not a real part of the murder scheme and a deal had been made with prosecutors. For breaking and entering he would be having court at another date on his charges but he would have to testify at Martha's trial.

The doorbell rang and Amy came in carrying fresh doughnuts. She poured herself a cup of coffee and sat down with me. We kissed and discussed the trial while we ate. She came to take me to get a new car. I was getting excited about it feeling safe with all the bad guys in jail but I would still have to be on the lookout for any of Jack's henchmen.

I went through several SUV's until I found one that would fit the family comfortably. Maybe wishful thinking but hopefully we could take trips or go camping or whatever families do.

I bought a large metallic blue Dodge SUV with all leather inside. The seats could be laid down and made into beds, or they were removable. I talked to the salesman to be sure that all the comforts were there, every little bell and whistle were put on it including a small TV in the back seat. The storage area under the back seats was enormous and should hold whatever we needed. I just know this is okay with Amy. Hopefully the family would agree.

I drove toward home feeling great about everything. Stopping by the police station to show off my new vehicle. Amy was very surprised. I told her that I would explain later. The cops came out and had a look too.

Sunday arrived with great excitement. I found my way around the grill and how to work with it. I started the charcoal burning, leaving it to heat up while I went inside to the kitchen and started going through all the bags I had brought with me. I set out the ingredients for my barbecue sauce. The ribs were in the refrigerator all ready to throw on the fire. The kids had not arrived as yet. I was getting more nervous as the time seemed to go slow.

One of the girls hollered from the living room and Amy left to meet her. Soon they were back and I was introduced to Carol, Pat and Mike. Mike was a bit on the bashful side and tried to hide behind his Dad's legs while he peeked out at me. I smiled and played with him as he slowly left the safety of his dad's legs and came forward into room. We seemed to be instant friends. As I was getting the prepared ribs from the refrigerator and headed to the backyard, he fell in beside me, wanting to come with me and help. So away we went with him carrying the salt and pepper for me. I threw the ribs on the grill and went back into the kitchen for the sauce with Mike right with me. I asked Amy for a large piece of white paper. I fashioned a cook's hat from it, printing cook on the sides and placed it on Mike's head. He was a happy proud little boy and strutted around telling everyone that he was cooking. What a cute kid. I was basting the ribs and he thought he should too, so I lifted him up so he could reach the grill with the meat brush. He had to go tell his dad what he had done.

Going into the kitchen again he was met by Beth. Amy introduced Beth, Derek and their boys Pete and Gary to Tom. A very nice family. The family resemblance was certainly there. The boys had brought a plastic baseball and bat. We found ourselves in a ball game while the cooking was being finished. We tried not to bat very hard and we dropped the ball a lot but the boys had a great time.

The girls were setting the table and Amy was starting to bring out the salads and all the foods. I went inside and brought out my big platter. Filling it with the ribs, I set it in the middle of the table among all the great foods. I was immediately very hungry. Amy told us to sit down and help ourselves. I did not need to be told twice. Mike set right next to me. He was not going to let me get away. It sure made me feel good and I lost some of the nervous butterflies I had in my stomach. With my anxiousness gone, I was able to relax, visit, and enjoy everyone.

As usual the conversation got a round to the murder and all that had gone on. Each person was in agreement that Jack, Martha and Belmont should get the death penalty while the others should get life in prison. Everyone knew it all depended on the jury.

CHAPTER 16

Robert Devon had stopped in to talk with the detectives. He was told that he acted very suspicious during all of these happenings. He was asked many questions about his part in all of this. Why the special business card? Why did he show up after something had happened? They told him that he had to explain his part in this, in detail.

He told the same story, more or less that Martha had. His orders were to remain as much undercover as possible. He was trying to stay out of Jack's sight so as to be there for Sandra. His assignment was to keep watch over her and also to do what he could to bring Jack to justice. He was not quick enough to save her and felt very sorry but he would try to see that Jack got the death penalty.

Everyone was in agreement hoping they all got the death penalty. Tomorrow was the big day. Jack was to be tried first. An agreement had been made that as soon as Jack's trial was over, and he was sentenced, the FBI would step in, arrest him on federal charges, and transport him to McNeil

Island Federal Prison where he would be tried on federal charges before a grand jury. There he would wait until he was tried by a federal court for other crimes ranging from Murder. Grand Theft Auto, Narcotics, Jury Tampering, and other offenses across the country. The D.A. and the FBI promised that the death penalty would be in forced.

The courtroom was filled. Jack's trial had begun. Cab was called first as a prosecution witness. Jack tried to stand up, yelling obscenities at him. His attorney grabbed him and sat him back down just as a police officer came toward him. The judge was banging his gavel and calling for order. He was very belligerent but became quiet. Cab was asked to explain how he knew Jack Roma? He explained that he had been approached while playing pool at Boyd's Bar. Jack had given him Twenty-Five thousand dollars in a small manila envelope to kill Thomas Donavon and had promised him $25,000.00 if the job was finished right away. He acted surly and real mean and Cab knew not to cross him.

The trial went on with each side objecting and arguing. At some points the attorneys would become so embroiled that the Judge would bang his gavel, call them forward and put a stop to their arguments.

Cab was asked how his friends were involved? He replied that he had hired them to shoot up Donavon's car and make it look like a drive by shooting but Kip got trigger happy and starting shooting to soon. When asked about Russ, Jer and

Kip, he answered that Russ was his brother and Jer and Kip were friends. When the attorneys were finished asking him questions, the judge excused him and a bailiff came forward and walked him out of the court room.

Next Russ was put on the stand and asked the same questions. He just answered that he was with his brother. He did not know what was going to happen. He was just there. Under the circumstances, the D.A. and defense attorney excused him and he too was escorted out of the courtroom. Jer and Kip were called one by one, and each of them told more or less the same story. But unlike Russ, Cab had hired them to do the shooting. The defense attorney tried to make them out to be liars and druggies but the D.A. was right there to argue several relevant points.

Martha was called to the stand. She told everything that she had told us. She wanted Jack to be found guilty. After much questioning by both sides, she was excused. A police matron was standing by waiting. After her testimony, she was then delivered back to her jail cell to await her trial.

Jack sat silent with a nasty stare on his face looking at each and every witness as they came and went. I was told that I would not be needed in Jack's trial but I would be needed at Martha's trial and possibly at the trial of the others. After days of testimony, the trial was over and the Jury was sent to deliberate.

Amy and I went to grab something to eat. We did not know when the jury would be done deliberating. We took our time and finally went back to the court room, waited and visited with other law enforcement. It seemed like forever before a bailiff came to tell us that the jury had retired for the night. Amy suggested that we meet at the police station in the morning early. Amy had asked the D.A. to call the precinct as soon as he heard something and he agreed.

Amy called at 8 o'clock to let me know the jury was in. I met her at the courtroom. Being one of the first to arrive she had found seats fairly close to the front where we could see and hear the proceedings. The Judge came in and we all stood. Then we were told to be seated. The jury was brought in and seated. The door beside the judge's chamber opened and Jack in handcuffs and leg chains, and surrounded by several officers, was escorted into the courtroom and seated at the defense table where his attorney waited. The judge opened court and asked the bailiff to get the jury findings from the jury foreman. After looking the paper over, the judge asked the jury foreman if they had reached a decision and was told that they had. Jack and his attorney stood as the judge read the findings. Jack had been found guilty of all charges, knowing it meant the death penalty. The judge asked Jack if he had anything he wanted to say. Jack remained quiet, showing his nasty stare. The judge asked him again and again, and there was no answer. His attorney suggested that he answer the judge with either with a yes or a no. Using obscene language and with hate in his voice, he began to rant and rave. An officer immediately sat him down and he was told in a harsh manner to be quiet. The judge set the date of sentencing for two weeks from that date. The court was told that Jack would be turned over to the FBI immediately after his sentencing. The judge excused the jury with the thanks of the court and then he adjourned. At this point the officers again surrounded Jack and escorted him back to his solitary confinement at the jail to await sentencing.

Early before Jack's trial was slated to begin, Martha met with the prosecutors. For her testimony at Jack's trial, she agreed to plead guilty to all the charges and would be given twenty five years to life. She could ask for parole after twenty five years. The death penalty would not come up. The D.A., the defense attorney and Martha met in the judge's chambers. The judge asked the D.A. for an explanation for the request. After the D.A. explained the situation, the judge asked the defense attorney if he agreed to this and was told yes. The judge then said there would not be a trial as the defendant had pled guilty. He asked her if she agreed to this and she said that she did. He went on to list her crimes and found her guilty of all crimes and repeated to her what the prosecutor had agreed on. She was led away under guard, and would later be sentenced to five years to life, serving her time at Purdy Women's prison.

Cab, Russ, Jer and Kip were all convicted of Attempted Murder, Weapon Charges, Grand Theft Auto and Public Endangerment. Because of their testimonies at Jack's trial, they were each sentenced to life in prison with possible parole after twenty five years. Then, they were transported to Walla Walla State Prison where they would all be separated and serve out their sentences. They would be off the streets for a very long time.

I was at home, and made coffee and then went to look around and check the apartments. I stood in the hallway facing Sandra's and Martha's apartments. I thought back over the events of the past few weeks. I never would have thought all these events could happen right here in the apartments. I will never forget and I grieve for Sandra, but the people involved with her murder will pay with their lives. Since I do not have a known relative of Sandra's or Martha's, I will be having an estate sale of all their belongings. The proceeds will be donated to the Seattle Gospel Mission for their kitchens, in Sandra's name.

As I returned to my apartment, the aroma from the coffee came through the hallway, smelling enticing and relaxing. It was great to relax and sip coffee.

I went into the bedroom, standing in front of the mirror, I adjusted my tie and put on my suit jacket. I heard Amy calling me from the living room. We have to be at the courthouse in an hour. The judge is waiting to marry us.